Moonstone Promise

2
DIAMOND
SPIRIT

Moonstone Promise

KAREN WOOD

ALLEN&UNWIN

Allen & Unwin
83 Alexander Street
Crows Nest NSW 2065
Australia
Phone: (61 2) 8425 0100
Fax: (61 2) 9906 2218
Email: info@allenandunwin.com
Web: www.allenandunwin.com

Cataloguing-in-Publication details are available from the
National Library of Australia www.trove.nla.gov.au

ISBN 978 1 74237 316 4

Cover photo by Bill Bachman/Wildlight
Cover and text design by Ruth Grüner
Set in 11.3 pt Apollo MT by Ruth Grüner
This book was printed in January 2014 at Griffin Press,
168 Cross Keys Road, Salisbury South, South Australia 5106, Australia

7 9 10 8 6

The paper in this book is FSC® certified.
FSC® promotes environmentally responsible,
socially beneficial and economically viable
management of the world's forests.

For Jack Bradley and Matty Glenn

1

'LAST ONE!' yelled Tom, as he sent a bale of prime lucerne tumbling off the back of the semitrailer.

Luke let it fall to the ground end-first. It bounced, then toppled onto its side with a thud. He stabbed his hay hooks into it and with one last surge of energy heaved it up to the top of the stack, where Lawson was arranging the bales tightly in a crisscross pattern.

'That it?' yelled Lawson.

'Yep,' Luke shouted back, hanging the hooks onto the beam that ran along the wall of the shed. He was dripping with sweat, itchy from the tiny stalks and dust, and his muscles ached, but he felt great. 'That oughta keep their bellies full for a while,' he said, looking up at the mountain of hay.

Lawson scrambled down the side of the stack like a mountain goat and brushed the loose green leaves from the front of his shirt. 'Eight hundred bales. I'm knackered!'

'Chuck us the water bottle, Luke.' Tom let himself down onto the edge of the empty trailer and sat with his legs hanging over.

Luke tossed a bottle to him, and looked around for a broom. He swept the loose hay into a pile, then leaned on the rake while he looked around the hay shed.

It had taken the three of them all weekend to empty it out for the hay. There'd been stacks of old tyres, drums of diesel, old snigging chains and the skeletal remains of a vintage car. Beneath that they'd found rags, dead mice and mounds of composted God-only-knew-what. They'd salvaged anything worthy, taken the rest to the tip, shovelled up the rotting remains and pressure-hosed the concrete floor. In its place stood the proud castle of leafy green lucerne, enough to last the winter.

Luke got back to sweeping. The sooner he could get this cleaned up, the sooner he could go and find Harry. The old man had been looking brighter this morning. He might even come and do the afternoon feeds. There was a tonne of things Luke wanted Harry to look at down the paddock. He wanted to show him that filly's leg and ask what he wanted done with the western fence.

'Hey, Luke!' Tom's yell from outside stopped him in his tracks. 'Luke, quick! The stallion's out!'

Luke dropped the broom and ran around the side of the truck. He'd been the last person to go into Biyanga's yard, but couldn't have left the gate unlatched; he was meticulous about that sort of thing. He stopped and glanced around quickly for Harry's good stallion.

Everything was at peace. The mares were grazing, Grunter the pig snuffled at a leaky water trough and chooks pecked busily beneath feed bins. All seemed to be as it should at Harry's place.

Luke looked up towards the stables and a blast of water hit him with so much force it nearly knocked him over. His arms flew up to shield his face and he stumbled backwards, coughing and spluttering while the jets of water hammered him all over.

Tom screamed with laughter and kept blasting him.

'You're *dead*, Tommo!' Luke spluttered, rushing at his friend and groping for the hose.

Tom had been playing jokes on him all weekend: dead mice in his workboots, a broken chair leg strategically concealed. It was about time Luke got his own back.

He fought Tom for the hose, knocking him to the ground and shoving his fingers up into his armpits so hard that Tom squealed like a girl and let go. The hose snaked wildly, twisting in the air and sending arcs of water from one end of the yard to the other. A jet slashed across Lawson's chest as he walked out of the shed to see what the commotion was. A look of thunder crossed his face.

3

'Now you've done it.' Luke pinned Tom's arms down into the mud. 'Lawson's gonna get you *bad*.' He let go of Tom and stepped aside as Lawson, bigger than the two of them put together, stormed towards them.

'He's all yours,' grinned Luke. Tom squirmed in a pool of mud and looked sheepishly at Lawson.

'Get that hose turned off and stop wasting water, Tom. You oughta know better than that.'

'Sorry, Lawson,' said Tom, struggling to keep a straight face.

Luke grabbed for the wayward hose and kinked it while Tom pulled himself up and walked towards the tap. Luke followed, and as soon as it was tightly shut off he made a grab for the designer undies peeping out the top of Tom's jeans and gave his mate the biggest, hardest wedgie he could. 'Take that back to boarding school with you,' he laughed, and bolted for the stables, leaving Tom cursing and clutching the back of his jeans.

Harry was in the stable aisle. Luke stopped in his tracks, dripping wet, and stared at him. Harry: the big charismatic man with the twinkling blue eyes, wheezy cough and leathery skin. He looked so frail and colourless.

'Hi, Harry,' Luke said, shaking his arms off.

'How'd you go with the hay?' The old man fumbled in his pockets and brought out a pouch of tobacco.

'All stacked,' said Luke.

'Any good?'

'Nice and fresh, leafy. It's good.'

'Find that loose stallion?'

Luke startled. 'I thought . . .' He looked over Harry's shoulder. Biyanga stood in his stable, chewing on a mouthful of hay.

Harry chuckled. 'Tom got you a beauty.'

Luke watched Tom walk into the building, still pulling at his backside. 'I got him better.'

'You nearly cut me in half,' grumbled Tom, as he walked to the feedroom. 'Feeding up?'

Luke pulled the ute keys out of his pocket and jangled them. 'Sunday, they all get hay!' He looked hopefully at the old man, who stood there hand-rolling a ciggie. 'Gonna come, Harry?'

Harry slowly ran his tongue along the edge of the cigarette paper and then rolled it shut between his fingers and thumbs. He shrugged. 'Yeah, Annie'll kill me if she sees me smoking this thing.'

Luke's heart leapt. Harry hadn't been down to the paddock for over a week. He must be feeling a lot better. Luke walked over to the old man and took him gently by the arm.

Harry shook him off. 'No need for that,' he grumbled and shuffled towards the ute, taking big, laboured breaths. 'You drive.'

Luke ran to yank the door open for him, then jumped into the driver's seat. 'You're in the back, Tom!'

Tom came out of the feedroom looking sharp in a fresh change of city clothes. 'Can't,' he said, slinging a pack over his shoulder. 'Dad's here.' A horn honked out the front of the property. 'See you in a few weeks, okay?'

Luke slumped. It had been good having Tom around for the weekend. 'Thanks for the help with the hay,' he said, closing the door and winding the window down.

'Look after my horse for me!' Tom ran to the gate.

Luke waved out the window and then glanced at Harry, who was lighting up – unbelievable. Luke crunched the ute into gear, pumped the accelerator, then hung his head and half his body out the window while reversing to the top of the laneway. After opening the gate, he kept reversing, all the way down.

At the bottom he pulled his head back into the cabin. Harry stared at him with a puzzled expression.

'Something with the crankshaft,' shrugged Luke. 'Lawson's gonna look at it this week.' He yanked on the handbrake.

Harry raised an eyebrow, then dragged in a lungful of smoke, wheezing and spluttering as he exhaled.

Luke tried not to listen to it. How a man with lung cancer could keep sucking on those things was beyond him. 'I tightened up all those fences, replaced two of the

6

posts,' he said, pointing to the other side of the mares' paddock. 'They came up real good. And I fixed the ball-cock in the trough. It runs heaps better now.'

Harry kept coughing. Luke walked to the back of the ute and grabbed a whole bale of hay. He'd show Harry the cut on that filly's leg once he got them all fed. It wasn't healing right. Out in the paddock, he spread the bale out between the horses, then headed back for another one.

Harry was slumped over in the front of the ute with his eyes closed.

'Oh no, Harry.' Luke broke into a run, leapt the fence in a bound and yanked the door open. In the front seat, Harry took long squeaky pulls for air. The ciggie smouldered quietly, burning into his trousers. Luke grabbed it and flicked it out of the car. 'You okay, Harry?'

Harry didn't respond.

Luke gave him a gentle shake. 'Harry?'

The old man squeezed his eyes shut and sucked harder for air.

Luke slammed the door and ran to the driver's side. He crunched and crunched at the gears, but couldn't get it into first. 'Hang in there, Harry.' He pressed the horn on the steering wheel and a limp whine came out. Leaping out and dragging the gate open, he yelled '*Lawson!*' as loudly as he could. 'Hold on, Harry!'

Luke reversed at full speed into the mares' paddock,

scattering the horses, then hit the brakes and sent the ute into a one-eighty. He reversed back out, not bothering with the gate and flew backwards straight up the laneway, bumping and banging the whole way. Harry slumped onto the dashboard, fighting for breath.

He yelled for Lawson again as he entered the stable yard. Lawson came running. He opened Harry's door and immediately reached into his pocket for his phone.

'He can't breathe!' said Luke, as he leaned across and helped Harry to sit back. The old man's eyes were wide open and his neck strained. 'He's not getting any air in at all!'

While Lawson gave the nearest crossroad to the triple-0 service, Annie ran up behind him. She pulled him out of the way and knelt down by Harry. 'What've you done to yourself, love?' she said gently, holding her husband up. She looked across at Luke. 'Was he sneaking fags again?'

Luke froze. He didn't want to dob on the old man.

'Was he or not?' snapped Annie.

Luke nodded.

Annie set her lips tight and shook her head. 'You've got lung cancer, you old fool!' She pulled a puffer from her pocket and tried to squirt it into Harry's mouth. 'Try to breathe in, love.' She turned to Lawson. 'How long till they get here?'

'Twenty minutes.'

'He won't last twenty minutes!' Annie began frantically squeezing the inhaler at Harry's lips. 'Come on, love, *breathe*.'

'Help me sit him up,' said Lawson. Luke reached across the ute and helped to hold the old man up.

'Don't you give up, Harry!' said Lawson. 'Keep trying. Get that air in.'

Harry lifted his head and sucked for air.

'That's it, relax your shoulders, stay calm,' said Lawson. 'Keep trying, the ambulance is coming, you just gotta keep sucking in what air you can, old man.'

2

WEEKS LATER, Luke lay in his bed with his arms over his face. Harry's snore, jagged and erratic, vibrated along the hallway, reaching his room and rattling at the door. Luke hated the snoring. No matter how many times he told himself it was just Harry, that sound made the walls close in on him. Memories of other foster homes came crashing into his head. He rolled onto his side, pulling a thin cotton sheet over his bare shoulder. He covered his head with his arms again and tried to think of something better.

But it didn't work. Another snore ripped through the night, choked and raspy.

Luke didn't know what was going to happen once Harry's old lungs finally gave out. All he knew was that there would be some big changes, but no one had talked about what those changes might be. To do so would be premature, disrespectful. Until now, everyone had carried on as usual. Harry had faded more and more into the background while Luke and Lawson had tried to keep the property running for him.

Everything will work out. Harry won't let anything bad happen to me.

Luke closed his eyes and tried to sleep again, but his legs wouldn't stay still. Eventually, he pushed the sheet off and sat up. It was a hot night and he wore only a pair of shorts. He peered out the window, then gently slid it open and swung his legs over the sill. Outside, crickets chirruped. A horse snorted softly down at the stables. Biyanga: he recognised the deep, throaty tone of a stallion.

On the mossy pavers of the courtyard lay a carpet of decomposing flowers from a big old jacaranda tree. Annie and Harry had afternoon tea under that tree in the summer months. It was their special place. Luke had seen them kissing on more than one occasion, just a bit of a peck, but it was still all lovey-dovey, which was kind of gross. They were so . . . *old*. Too old for that sort of carry-on, anyway.

He heard one last snore as he closed the window and padded across the courtyard. He came to the back wall of the stables and slipped through the small door leading into the building.

The stable aisle was cool and dark. Biyanga sniffed at

the air and gave a low rumbling greeting as Luke walked softly along the concrete towards Legsy's stall. Other horses shuffled through the thick wood shavings, their joints clicking quietly. They peered over the stable doors with curious faces.

Luke held out his hand and found Legsy's muzzle. It was cool and whiskery and nipped lazily at his empty hand. 'Hey,' he whispered and ran his hand over the colt's warm, satiny neck. Legsy ran his muzzle up over Luke's shoulder and sniffed at his hair. It gave him goosebumps and brought a smile to his face. Legsy was one of the first horses he had ever gentled; they were best of buddies. He wore a red rug, the prize they had won together at the last campdraft. 'Did I wake you up?' Luke mumbled. 'Lucky fella, at least you can sleep.'

He walked to the feedroom, pulled the door across and slid into the blackness. Groping his way to the back wall, he found a pile of horse rugs in the corner. He pulled them up in armfuls, carried them out into the aisle and tossed them on the ground. Then he flopped down into them and breathed in the salty horse sweat, the earthy dried mud, the lucerne and pine. A tiny breeze ran along the cool concrete and over his bare shoulder. The steady munch of a horse chewing hay, the shift of hooves over the soft wood shavings, the faint whistle of Legsy's breathing rocked him gently into sleep.

A clatter of horseshoes on concrete jolted Luke into the new day. Biyanga called loud throaty whinnies and banged at his stable door with his front hoof. Legsy squealed excitedly. Luke pulled himself out of the pile of horse rugs and cursed himself for sleeping in. It was hot already and a pulsing headache thudded against his skull.

Grace Arnold, Harry's thirteen-year-old niece, sat on a grey horse wearing old jeans, a singlet and black helmet. Although she was a slob, a tomboy, a loudmouth and general pain in the butt, she was about the bravest girl rider Luke had ever met. She would get on anything. The horse she sat on now looked young and gangly – probably a breaker, judging by the big old poley saddle she was sitting in, and the way it shifted about nervously, scraping its metal shoes over the slippery concrete.

'What are you doing?' she asked. 'Did you sleep there?'

'What does it look like?' Luke got to his feet and began bundling up the rugs.

'No need to be snappy,' said Grace, slipping off the horse and tethering it.

Luke knew he shouldn't be short with her, but his head was pounding. He carried the rugs into the feedroom.

'Excuse me,' he said, as he pushed past her, but not before he caught her eyes running over his broken, lumpy ribs. He usually kept them well hidden.

'Why did you sleep down here?' Grace asked again. 'Is there a sick horse or something?'

'Legs was a bit colicky,' he lied. 'Can you feed up?' He stalked off to get some breakfast. It was Sunday – his day off.

Back at the house, he didn't bother showering. Standing with the fridge door open, he skulled the last of the juice and chucked the empty carton in the bin. He scoffed ten honey-smothered Weet-Bix, two more than comfortably fit in his stomach, and went to his room to get changed. He could hear Harry wheezing from the end of the hallway as he pulled a T-shirt over his head. It didn't sound as if the oxygen tank was doing him much good.

He probably wouldn't see the old man until lunchtime. That was the only time Luke saw him now: after the horses were fed and worked, and all the odd jobs were done. Annie rarely left Harry's side. She sat next to his bed, adjusting the tanks, fiddling about with the sheets and bringing him cups of tea which he never drank. Around midday, Luke usually went in there and gave him a morning report on the horses. The last couple of days, though, Harry had seemed uninterested.

Luke decided to quickly pop his head in and see if he

was feeling any better this morning. He'd missed the old man's gruff humour and reassuring manner, even though they never really talked about much – just horses, mostly. He knocked quietly on the door.

A voice mumbled.

Luke pushed the door open and saw Harry pulling himself upright onto the side of the bed, facing out the window.

'That you, Lawson?'

'It's Luke,' he said, walking around to where the old man could see him. 'Just wanted to see if you were feeling any better today.' He sat in the chair that had been strategically placed for visitors.

'Bloody freezing,' said Harry. 'Pass me my jumper, will you?'

Luke helped him to sling it around his shoulders, noting how hot he felt himself. After a short silence, Harry spoke again. 'Can you put Bunyip in the paddock where I can see him?'

'Bunyip?' Luke questioned. Bunyip was Harry's first horse – he had died years ago. 'Don't you mean Biyanga?'

'Yeah, yeah, the stallion,' Harry corrected himself.

'He's just finishing his feed, then I'll put him out.'

Harry stared at the window. Outside, his property stretched over acres of riverfront land, patched into paddocks, sloping gently down to the water. But Harry didn't seem to see past the glass. 'Gonna see old Bunyip again soon,' he mumbled.

He'd been saying this for days and it seemed to make him feel better, so Luke went along with it. 'Gonna pull some big scores on that old fella, hey, Harry,' he said, trying to sound cheerful. 'Sounds like a pretty sharp horse.'

'The best,' mumbled Harry. He hacked out a horrible wheezing cough and reached for a hanky. 'I want to ask you a big favour,' he whispered.

'Anything,' said Luke. 'You name it.'

'Ride the stallion for me,' said Harry. 'Right up the front. When they . . . you know. It'd mean a real lot to me.'

'Biyanga?'

Harry nodded and wheezed into his hanky again.

'Don't you want Lawson to?'

Lawson was Harry's only blood son. Surely he would lead the procession. He would ride Harry's good horse.

'No, I want you to ride him,' said Harry.

'Me?' Luke clarified again. Maybe Harry meant Ryan. Ryan was his stepson, Annie's boy. 'As in Luke?'

'I know who you are,' grumbled Harry.

'Won't the others mind?' Being fostered, Luke always considered himself to be at the bottom of the pecking order.

'I already told them what I want.' Harry sounded short.

Luke's breath caught in his throat as he thought of what Harry's funeral might be like. He hadn't let himself think about it up until now. None of it seemed quite real. 'Yeah, yeah, absolutely. I'd be . . . honoured.' Talking about this was weird. It was wrong.

Harry nodded. 'Better rest now.'

Luke helped him back down onto the pillow and the old man shut his eyes. 'I'll get Annie,' Luke told him.

Harry nodded again without speaking, his face tight with pain.

Luke passed Lawson on the way out of the bedroom. He didn't mean to push past him, but he had to get out of there before he was swallowed up and drowned. Outside the room, he leaned against the closed door, taking a moment to get himself together. This was it. It was really happening. He was going to lose Harry.

Inside the room, he could hear Harry and Lawson talking.

'Yeah, whatever, the foster kid can ride him,' he heard Lawson say. 'Have you sorted out his arrangements?'

Luke strained to hear Harry's answer. He only caught a wheezy mumble.

'Jesus, Harry.' Lawson sounded annoyed.

There was another wheezy mumble.

'Well, did you tell *him* that?'

Tell me what?

'Oh, so I have to tell him? I've told you, if you want to bring in every stray kid you find, you can sort it all out. I don't want a whole lot of caseworkers and child safety officers going through every inch of my life. You know what'll happen if you leave all that to me.'

Dread seeped, warm and sickly, through Luke's body.

'Don't let them take me back, Harry,' he whispered. 'Please don't do that to me. This is my home now.'

3

LUKE PUSHED THROUGH the front door and a blast of hot air hit him in the face. It wasn't until he was in Legsy's stable and standing with his arms around the colt's big, solid neck that his head stopped spinning.

Biyanga and the other horses were already out in the yards. Grace must have fed them. In the yard closest to the stables Luke could see Nosey, Legsy's twin brother. Harry reckoned it was rare for mares to give birth to healthy twin foals. Usually one died before full term. Both these colts were spectacular, the only minor flaw in Nosey being a slightly clubbed foot. Harry had gelded him and sold him to Tom. But Legsy was too good to geld. He was already showing a lot of promise at campdrafting.

Luke slipped a bridle over Legsy's ears and led him out of the stable, wishing Tom would hurry up and get back from boarding school. His practical jokes and wrestling would be a welcome change from the gloom and doom.

Luke kicked off his thongs, vaulted onto Legsy bareback, and walked him down the road.

He turned the colt off into some trees and rode down a well-worn track that came out onto the river flats — long green stretches of land that followed the river and connected all the properties in Coachwood Crossing. Legs danced about beneath him, so he took hold of a chunk of mane and let him have his head. The colt lurched into a canter, then stretched into a rolling, thunderous gallop through the knee-high grass. The wind rushed over Luke's face, and the wide open sky let him breathe again. Legsy pigrooted, and he laughed.

He didn't need to tell Legs where to go. The colt headed straight for the tree-line and pushed past some bushes down to the bank of the river. There was a sandy spot with hoofmarks all over it, where Legs lowered his nose and sniffed his way to the water's edge. He drank a few quick mouthfuls, then ventured in further and began smashing playfully at the water with his front leg.

The colt buckled at the knees and dropped. Luke jumped off to the side and let him roll in the cool river, grinding his back into the grainy sand, his huge black belly in the air and his legs waving clumsily about. Finally Legs scrambled to his feet, shook like an enormous dog and nipped at Luke's face. Luke smiled and gave him a rub on the forehead, then led him to a tree and tethered him.

A tree had fallen into the river, creating a dam a little further down. Luke took off his shirt and clambered along the boulders like a monkey. He climbed up onto a rock platform and dived into the deepest part, letting the water swallow him up and cover him in its silky coolness, soothing the tension away.

He floated on his back, staring up at the trees. Bands of silver light streaked through them, bouncing off the water that rippled over his chest. On his right side, his ribs stuck out in ugly lumps, five of them.

I'm not going to another foster home. Not ever. I'm done with that.

He thought back to the time when he'd first met Harry, through a six-week horse-gentling program run by a youth organisation. Luke was a busted-up, angry kid. Harry was a horse trainer.

The stallion had been crazy, screaming and prancing, pulling both front feet off the ground and tossing his long black mane. He was blacker than black and evil-looking. When Luke saw Harry pull that wild six-hundred-kilo animal out of the stable, all snorting and farting and screaming, he had nearly crapped in his pants. With the stallion carrying on behind him, Harry had walked quietly as if nothing was happening, chewing at a toothpick, inspecting a fingernail and even stopping to empty a stone out of his boot.

Luke had backed away, out of reach of those powerful hind legs, but Harry had spoken to him without even looking at him. 'Chuck me that hoof pick, kid,' he said. Then he turned and picked that enormous animal's foot up off the ground.

That was all Harry had said to him for the entire day. Luke hadn't even known what a hoof pick was. He had just stood there, staring, noticing that despite the stallion's noise, it never pulled away from the rope, or harmed a hair on that old man's head – not that there were many.

The stallion seemed to know exactly where old Harry was at all times, and respected his space. That was the first time Luke had ever seen such power and strength bridled through respect rather than force. It was a strange and fascinating energy between the horse and the old man.

Luke had watched every day from the fence, until he worked out what a hoof pick was and began taking it to the old fella with arm outstretched, not wanting to get too close to the big hairy animal. 'Chuck us the clinch cutters,' the old man had said on another day. Luke had passed him several different tools before getting the right one.

Back then, Harry had never tried to be a father or a mentor or a leader. He just demonstrated a better way, quietly going about his business, letting Luke come at him with questions in his own time. 'How do you control them?' Luke had finally asked. 'How do you break them when they're wild like that?' That was when their friendship really began.

After days of running his hands over them, winning their trust, working with them, Luke would sit on his bed looking through his photos, trying to remember who he was before he got lost in the black hole.

In his favourite, his real mum sat on a horse with him in front of her. Her arms were wrapped around him, a grinning little boy, keeping him safe, holding the reins and smiling for the camera. She was the most beautiful woman he had ever seen. Young, fit, barefoot, in shorts and a singlet, with shoulder-length thick hair – he didn't know what colour, because it was a black-and-white shot.

His real dad was only in a couple of photos, riding a horse in both. Luke had tortured himself with the same question for years.

Why did he give me up?

In the end, Luke had stopped torturing himself about it. It wasn't going to change anything. His real dad hadn't wanted him after his mum died, for whatever reason, and that was that. Harry filled that gap now.

But it was the photos that had made him want to give the horse-gentling program a go. He knew that somehow horses were a part of his make-up, even though he had felt no connection with them before he met Harry. And he was right. Once he did connect with them, he knew he could never let them go. Horses were a part of him and always would be.

Harry had seen it in him, too, and asked him to stay on. It had taken a lot of organising on Annie's part, but eventually Harry and Annie ended up officially fostering him. The last few years had been the best of Luke's life.

He closed his eyes and lay there floating in the river with his arms out, thinking about those years – he didn't know how long for.

4

WHEN LUKE EVENTUALLY pulled himself out of the river, he jumped back on Legsy and rode further along the river flats. He didn't want to go home yet. When he passed the back of Lawson's property, he pulled the colt back to a walk and looked searchingly up through the hill paddock. He wondered if she'd be there, sitting under the mango tree.

Jess. He remembered when he had first came across her. She was the girl he had seen riding over the river flats, on a buckskin appaloosa. The small horse was striking: golden, with a thick black mane and tail, and silver spots all over its rump. The girl rode so easily, often bareback and barefoot. Cantering, always cantering, never walking, so Luke never had an opportunity to ride out across the big grassy stretches and say 'Hi' to her.

Then she had turned up at Harry's place one day

with the biggest black eye he had ever seen. He hadn't recognised her at first. She was riding a bike and trying to hide her face. But he recognised her hair, golden-brown, silky and messy. She was quiet, withdrawn, as if she'd had the spirit knocked out of her.

She too found refuge at Harry's place, and as she started to heal, Luke watched her downcast eyes gradually become feisty and determined again. Her serious mouth had a one-sided smirk that flashed so quickly across her face you could miss it. He found himself watching for it and sometimes she would catch him, holding his gaze for just a second. But then Grace or Shara would break the moment with a loud yell, an excited suggestion or a pushy demand.

'Doesn't matter how much you stare at it,' he yelled out to Jess now. 'It's not gonna grow any faster.'

Jess, wearing an old flanny and jeans, smiled and waved as she jumped up and ran over to the fence. 'I saw it kicking,' she called out before she got there. 'I could see a little hoof popping out the side of her belly. It was so cute!'

'I still can't believe you're getting a foal out of that mare for two hundred bucks,' he said.

'Two hundred and forty-six,' she corrected him.

Lawson's mare, Marnie, had fallen pregnant to a runaway stallion one crazy night in the outback, months ago. The horses had all escaped from a campdraft, and everyone had gone out looking for them. But only he and Jess had seen the min min lights – three of them, appearing out of nowhere and buzzing around the mares.

Jess reckoned they were spirits, ghosts, or some crazy mixed-up stuff to do with her first horse, Diamond, who had been destroyed after an accident. When she saw those lights seemingly disappear into Marnie's belly, she was convinced that Diamond had been reincarnated. She persuaded Lawson to sell her the foal for a pittance. And ever since, she'd been walking on sunshine.

'Hoping for a filly or a colt?' asked Luke.

'A filly,' Jess said, 'so I can breed from her one day.'

'Then you can spend another year sitting under a tree,' he teased.

Jess spent hours sitting under that mango tree staring at the mares – whole days, in fact. She had beaten a track along the river flats to Lawson's property to visit her favourite horse, Wally, and to check on Marnie's belly size. The mare wasn't due for weeks yet but it was all Jess ever talked about.

She took a swipe at Luke's foot and laughed. 'I like watching them. Anyway, I don't have a horse to ride. Dodger's foot still isn't right.'

'You know you can ride any of Harry's horses.'

'How is he?'

'Who, Harry?' Luke looked down. 'Not good. Tired. Cranky.'

'How about Annie?'

Luke just shrugged. 'Wanna come for a ride?' He gestured at Legsy's rump.

'Where to?'

Luke thought about it. 'Mossy Mountain?' It was the biggest mountain in the district, with a winding trail through palm forests and fern-covered cliffs. It took two hours to ride to the top. The view was amazing.

'Does he double?'

'Dunno,' Luke grinned, 'only one way to find out.'

'What if he bucks?'

'I s'pose we'll fall off.'

Jess climbed through the fence. 'I'm game.'

He held out an arm, and she grabbed it, springing up behind him. Legsy instantly lurched sideways. Jess squealed and clung to Luke's waist, nearly dragging him off.

'Get your feet out of his flanks,' he said, pulling the colt around.

'They're not *in* his flanks,' cried Jess.

'We just got to get him used to us both. Give him a pat on the rump.'

Jess leaned back and gave the colt a loud slap on the

rump, making him startle and jump forwards. 'Whoa!' she screamed.

'Not like that!' said Luke, grabbing at Legsy's reins.

'I thought this horse doubled,' laughed Jess.

'I thought you could ride!' he answered.

'Who told you that? It's a vicious lie!'

He felt two hands push into his back, then turned to see her somersaulting backwards over Legsy's rump and landing on her feet on the ground.

'Yeah, right.' Jess could ride all right. She was small and agile and brilliant at vaulting; she'd ridden in mounted games with her best friend Shara for years. Luke could tell she was stirring Legsy up on purpose.

'Try again?' she asked, climbing up onto the fence. 'Back him up.'

Luke reined Legsy's rump towards the fence. Jess patted him, more gently this time. 'Easy, fella.'

Legsy snorted and shifted about, unsure.

'Gee, he's nervous,' said Jess. 'Who broke him in? They did a crap job.'

'Me,' said Luke, indignant. 'You getting on, or you just gonna do clown tricks all day?'

Jess leapfrogged onto Legsy's rump and wriggled up onto his back.

Luke let the colt's head go, and they set off towards Mossy Mountain.

As they passed the Pettilow property, Legsy began nickering and prancing about beneath them. He let out a loud squeal. Out beyond the trees a brilliant white horse grazed along the river flats.

'Chelpie's out *again*,' said Luke. He had lost count of how many times he'd come across the mare and led her back to Katrina Pettilow's place. He had even fixed the fence a couple of times, without so much as a thank you from the Pettilows.

'She's always out,' said Jess. 'If I had my phone on me, I'd ring the ranger.'

'She just wants some green-pick,' said Luke. 'There's hardly any grass in her paddock, poor thing.'

'Katrina should look after her better,' said Jess. 'Look at her big wormy belly. She needs a good stomach-drench.' He felt Jess shudder behind him. 'Ugh, she's so . . . nasty, and weird. I don't know what it is about her.'

Like Jess, Luke couldn't quite put his finger on what it was about Chelpie. She was always on the outer. Other horses didn't like her and she didn't like them. But he had a soft spot for the little mare.

'She's been nicer lately,' he said, wondering what had brought about the change in the little horse. Maybe she just liked having so much grass to eat. 'She came up for a pat when I rode past the other day.'

'Yeah, well, she better not come near me,' said Jess.

'You hate her too.'

'She killed my horse, what do you expect?'

It was true. Chelpie had chased Jess's horse, Diamond, into a cattle grid and got her killed. Jess had every right to hate the mare.

'May as well leave her there,' he said, changing the subject. 'She'll only get out again.'

'Let's ride up along the creek.' Jess reached through from behind and took one of the reins. She turned Legsy back towards the river. 'We can swim at Hell's Hole on the way.'

They left Chelpie and followed the creek up a cool gully, through low-growing ferns. The colt's hooves sank into wet sand as they followed a narrow track along the side of the creek, ducked under low-hanging branches and squeezed through narrow passes. In some sections of the creek, they crossed wide flat stretches of river pebbles; in others they waded through deeper water. Then they left the creek and traversed the side of a mountain, scrambling over rocks and crossing fallen trees covered in moss. As they climbed the hill, the trees became smaller and the forest more open.

They rode in silence. It was like that with Jess. She

and Luke seemed to slip so easily into the same rhythm and pace. When she was around, Luke found the world an easy place to be.

At the top, they came to a clearing and stopped. The view caught Luke's breath every time. Dark gullies and mountains tumbled down into the valley, which was green and wide and flat. The Coachwood River, like a long ribbon, coiled and slithered in big loops, carrying life to the bordering properties. Farms, patched in all sizes and shapes, ran along the sides of the valley for as far as the eye could see.

'There's my place,' said Jess, pointing west along the valley. 'Dad's slashing the paddock – look, I can see him!' She waved and laughed. 'Hi, Dad!'

Luke looked out over Coachwood Valley. It was the first place in his life that had ever felt like home – the people, the different farms, the little bunch of shops and the huge freight trains that rattled through so often he barely noticed them anymore.

'There's mine,' he said, pointing in the other direction. Harry's place was easy to see: a perfect rectangle, cut into neat paddocks.

But it didn't look right. There were cars all around the house. Lawson's ute, Ryan's truck, Mrs Arnold's four-wheel drive, an ambulance, two other cars he didn't recognise. They were parked at strange angles all over the front grassy stretch, as if they'd pulled up in a hurry. Stanley Arnold's little brumby ute drove in and Luke could see him running towards the house.

The day around him went still.

'Something's wrong,' he said.

5

LUKE STOOD IN FRONT of the mirror in the hallway and tried to work out his tie. He was tall now, and lanky, despite trying his best to get some meat onto his bones. He ran his hands through his thick rusty hair, trying to smooth it down.

Lawson appeared in the mirror and held his hand out for the tie. Luke ripped it off and passed it to him.

Ask him. Ask him now.

No one had said anything about his future. Everyone was too devastated by Harry's sudden heart failure to think of anything else. Annie had barely surfaced from the bedroom. Lawson had been busy with funeral arrangements.

Through the mirror, Luke could see Ryan talking to Harry's sister, Mrs Arnold, in the kitchen. There was always tension in the house when Ryan came home. Lawson was only helping with the tie as an excuse to stay away from him, Luke was sure. He wasn't normally the attentive type. If Ryan and Lawson got through the wake without a punch-up, it would be a small miracle.

'Want Annie to take the rug, or are you going to carry it on the horse?' Lawson asked as he folded the tie into a knot and handed it back to Luke.

'I'll carry it on the horse,' said Luke, noosing it up under his collar and tucking his white shirt into his moleskins.

It was Annie's idea for everyone to put something special on the casket. Luke was going to put Legsy's prize rug over it. Without Harry, they never would have won it. He took a deep breath and felt as though he was going to his own funeral.

Lawson looked him over and nodded. 'You look pretty snappy.'

Luke looked at himself next to Lawson. Neither of them got dressed up very often. With the same moleskins, shirt and tie, they could almost pass for real brothers. 'Wish we were going to a B and S instead.'

Lawson smiled. 'Yeah.'

Annie emerged from her bedroom, wearing black. She looked shaky and pale. 'It's time to go,' she said quietly.

The showgrounds were full of people; there were hundreds of them. Luke sprang onto Biyanga's back and joined Ryan and Lawson, who were already mounted and waiting by the main gates. As he took his position at the front, the stallion pulled and snatched at the bit, agitated by all the commotion. It took some strength for Luke to hold him steady while he looked back along the long lines of horses and people, searching for Jess.

She was riding her good horse, Dodger, who had a special boot buckled over his bad hoof. Shara, Grace and Grace's older sister, Rosie, rode next to her. Luke waved to try to get Jess's attention. Grace saw him, he was sure, but she turned away. She'd be jealous that he was riding the stallion.

'Hey, buddy.' Tom rode up beside him on Nosey.

'Hey,' said Luke. 'You made it!'

'Wouldn't miss it,' said Tom. He looked sharp, as always, in black moleskins and a cobalt-blue shirt. Tom always looked sharp. His parents had way too much money. It was the root of all his supposed problems. Luke had met him at Harry's horse-gentling program, and despite their different backgrounds they had clicked. Tom was a shit-stirrer, but he was also generous. Luke had been the benefactor of all his excesses: clothes, saddles, techno-gadgets. He was wearing one of Tom's shirts today. Sometimes it was embarrassing how much stuff Tom gave him.

Before they had a chance to catch up, the hearse rolled slowly around the corner. The sight of the casket covered in flowers in the back of the vehicle tore at Luke's heart. Biyanga screamed, shuddering violently, and broke from under him, rearing, tearing the reins from his hands and nearly knocking him from the saddle.

'You okay?' Tom reached out to grab the stallion's reins.

Luke shook his head.

'You can let go, I got him,' Tom said quietly.

Luke heaved in a few raspy breaths and wiped angrily at his eyes.

'I'm okay,' he said, taking back the reins. 'All right, Biyanga,' he soothed.

He saw Lawson and Ryan ride towards the hearse and take their positions. Lawson waved him over. 'I better go. I'm s'posed to ride up the front,' he said to Tom.

'Catch up later, ay?'

'You bet.'

He rode up to Ryan and Lawson and took his position between them. This was how Harry wanted it: Luke, on Biyanga, flanked by his two sons. It struck him that Harry's request had more purpose than just giving him the honour of riding the stallion. He hadn't wanted any fights on this day. Luke eyed his two foster brothers. They were both big blokes and he wouldn't want to get stuck in the middle of them, that was for sure. But so far, Lawson seemed to be taking the lead and Ryan seemed to be keeping his mouth shut.

'Up this way,' said Lawson, reining his horse away.

Luke loosened the reins and let Biyanga take the lead out in front of the hearse. Lawson and Ryan rode up either side of him.

'There must be two hundred riders here,' Luke said to Ryan. 'There aren't as many riders as this at most drafts we go to.'

'He had a pretty long history with horses,' said Ryan. 'But yeah, I didn't expect this many.'

And he was at the very front. That was a big honour. That was pretty cool. Luke took up the reins a bit and asked Biyanga to arch his neck and walk proud while he sat a little straighter in the saddle.

The old coach-house was five kilometres out of town, in a large open field by the lake. It was a small timber building with a steeply pitched roof. A verandah ran around three sides and four small steps spilled down to the front path.

Lawson and Ryan dismounted and passed their reins to Luke. Other people arrived in cars and made their way to the coach-house. With the help of Stanley and a few other blokes, they placed the casket on a stand on the verandah. Annie, Mrs Arnold and other family members and friends seated themselves on chairs next to it. Riders sat on their horses or stood quietly while a minister spoke from the verandah.

Poems were read and songs sung. Lawson and Ryan made short speeches, and then several other people did too. It took a long time and it was hot. Finally, Lawson nodded to Luke, indicating that it was time to step forward and place his rug over the casket.

First Annie walked up and placed a small black velvet pouch, drawn closed with a yellow cord, on the casket. She stroked the lid of the casket with a shaky hand and walked back to her seat. As he handed his reins to Stanley Arnold and stepped forward, Luke heard the unmistakeable tune of 'Amazing Grace' swim through his ears from Ryan's slide guitar.

It gutted him. He stood staring blankly at the casket, letting the slow haunting guitar riffs waft in and out of him.

'Luke.'

He looked up at Jess. She was bawling. She took the rug and helped him to fold it neatly in half and hang it over the casket. Then he watched as she placed a green-and-gold striped tie on top, together with a small handful of black powdery soil.

'He lived like a gentleman, and he should die like a gentleman,' she whispered without looking at him.

Lawson put Harry's grubby old hat on the casket and then he picked up his father's banjo and joined Ryan. Some old guy Luke had never seen before pulled out a harmonica. It was the saddest music he had ever heard. One by one, other people walked forward and placed flowers, small brass horse statues, envelopes, prize ribbons, crucifixes, bridles, stockwhips, a small hip flask, a stubby of beer, all sorts of things, on the casket. One woman even put a black lacy bra on it. Luke shot a glance at Annie, who was actually chuckling.

Later, the family took the casket to the crematorium. It disappeared behind a small curtain and Harry was gone, before Luke even had a chance to get used to the idea.

The wake went on all night. Back at Harry's place, the arena was full of people, the lights were blazing and various people were playing guitars and singing. Mrs Arnold and Jess's mum passed platters of food around, but it soon ran out and people drove into town to fetch pizzas and hot chips.

It was okay for a while. Luke mingled with Tom, Jess and Rosie, but then some of the guests started getting drunk. The voices got louder and the guitars started sounding out of tune. There were empty bottles, cans and pizza trays all over the arena. People Luke didn't know ran up and down the stable aisle, spooking the horses. In the end, he and Tom let them all out in the paddock where they could get some peace.

'I'm getting out of here,' Luke said to Tom, as he bolted the door to Biyanga's empty stable.

'Me too,' said Tom. 'Dad wants to go. I'll catch up with you on the weekend, hey?'

Luke shrugged and tried to look casual. 'Yeah, maybe.'

'Why, you going somewhere?' asked Tom, hanging a halter on a hook in the aisle.

'Dunno, have to wait and see.'

Tom looked at him, puzzled. 'What's going on?'

'The department will have to check over my whole life again.'

Tom's face dropped. 'They can't take you away from here, can they?'

Luke shrugged again. 'I don't know.'

'Single people can't keep foster kids,' said Grace, appearing out of nowhere. 'That's what Rosie reckons. She reckons a case worker will probably come and take you back.'

There was a stunned silence.

'That's not true, Grace,' Tom said in an icy voice.

It wasn't true. Luke knew it wasn't, but he couldn't speak. He had an overwhelming urge to walk up to Grace and smack her right in her big, flappy, insensitive mouth. He turned and walked away instead.

'What?' he heard Grace say behind him. 'It's true. He's not adopted. He's just a foster kid.'

'You can really be the pits sometimes, Grace,' said Tom. 'Mate, stop,' he called after Luke.

Luke flung open the back door of the stables, marched into the courtyard and went directly to the punching bag that hung from the old jacaranda tree. He sank his fist into it so hard that it nearly snapped the tree branch.

'She doesn't know what she's talking about, Luke,' said Tom, catching up with him. 'Annie wouldn't let that happen.'

Luke punched the bag again. 'She's right. I heard Lawson and Harry talking.'

'What?'

Luke kept punching the bag.

'Oh, come on, Luke,' Grace said from the stable door. 'I'm sorry, okay?'

'I think you should go away, Grace,' said Tom. 'You've already said enough.'

'I'm not going anywhere,' said Grace, sounding suddenly heated. 'This is *my* family's place. Not yours, not his. Don't tell *me* to go away!'

'I think you're both just upset,' said Tom. 'It's been a big day for everyone.'

'Luke gets treated like royalty around here,' Grace whined. 'He gets all the good horses, while I ride all the crap ones. And who asked him to ride Biyanga at the funeral?'

Luke spun around to face her. '*Harry* asked me to, that's who,' he yelled. 'Have you got a problem with that?'

'Come on, guys,' said Tom soothingly. 'You're upset. Don't get into this now.'

But it was too late. Something in Luke had opened up, like a deep wound that had healed on the outside but was still festering way below. 'What's it to you that I rode the stallion?' he yelled at Grace. 'It's none of your business. That was between Harry and me!'

'None of *my* business? You're not even family. Not even blood,' she said, her voice rising. 'Someone in the family should have ridden him.' She burst into tears and ran from the stable building.

Luke froze, not game to move or speak. He could feel poison oozing from everywhere.

Tom put a hand out towards Luke's shoulder. 'Don't listen to her, mate. You know what she's like.'

Luke turned away from Tom and back to the punching bag, but no matter how hard he hit that thing, he could still hear the drunken voices from the arena. His old life,

43

snapping at his heels, as if it was coming to get him. The voices were getting louder and more obnoxious. He ripped off the starchy white shirt that clung to his body and kept punching.

'Take it easy, kid,' Lawson said from the door of the stables.

'*You* take it easy,' Luke panted, still swinging.

'I heard what Grace said to you,' said Lawson, stepping closer and holding out an arm.

Lawson shouldn't have kept talking. He should have known the rules and kept clear.

'Don't come near me, Lawson,' Luke yelled. 'I'm warning you, *get away from me*.'

'Enough, Luke.' Lawson wrapped his large arms around Luke's shoulders and tried to pull him away from the bag.

That's when Luke swung at him. He punched Lawson smack in the jaw and it felt fantastic, liberating, bringing a gush of relief that left him able to breathe again.

Until Lawson punched him back, fair in the mouth, sending him sprawling onto the pavers with a pain that was brilliant, pure and intense, like fire marching over his face.

Lawson shook out his fist. He spoke to Luke in a low, measured tone.

'She's right – you're not one of us. That's not how

we go about our business in this family.' He turned and walked towards the stable doorway, but stopped and looked back before he went through it. 'Young Grace is going through about as much pain as you at the moment, probably more. Harry was like a second father to her. Of course she was cut that you rode the stallion.'

Luke gazed up at Lawson, his head foggy. 'So I'm not a part of this family anymore, then?'

Lawson glared down at him. 'You wanna be a Blake, you gotta earn the name.' He turned and walked back into the feedroom, banging the door behind him.

6

LUKE STAGGERED TO the river, sank to his knees and scooped handfuls of water over his head and face, washing off the blood. His lip was swollen and his cheek felt puffy, but the swelling would go down in a couple of days. He knew that Lawson could have done much better if he'd wanted to; the fact that he'd held back was all the more insulting. But it wasn't the punch that stung the most.

You wanna be a Blake, you gotta earn the name.

The river churned in time with the churning in Luke's gut. He splashed more water over the back of his neck and let it run down his spine, then some more over his face and eyes, so he couldn't tell if he was crying or not.

'Luke.' It was Jess.

'Not now, Jessy,' he choked out. He didn't want her seeing him like this. He didn't want anyone seeing him like this: exposed, stripped bare of everything, his family, his dignity. He didn't even have a shirt on.

She was still standing there. He could feel her staring at him. 'Get away from me!' he yelled.

There was silence, and then he heard her walk away. He wanted to call out to her to come back. God, he didn't mean to say that to her. But he couldn't. If he tried to speak he knew nothing would come out but big sobs.

Maybe Lawson was right. He wasn't a Blake. He didn't belong around here at all.

He ran his hands into the coarse river sand and squeezed its coolness through his fingers. It felt good, comforting. He ran his hands in deeper, up to his elbows, and then began digging until he lay with his entire body encased in the watery river sand, and the familiar comfort of the Coachwood River.

Luke didn't know what time of night it was when he eventually hosed the sand off himself in the horse wash before heading back to the stables. He knew what he had to do.

Most of the people had gone home, except for a few at the far end of the arena. He heard Ryan's voice among them as he walked through the feedroom and out the door into the courtyard. He crawled through his bedroom window, and paused to listen before he opened the door and walked three steps up the hall and into the bathroom.

He stared at his bruised face in the mirror. There was dried blood around the corner of his mouth, and he had mud caked in his hair. He turned on the tap and squeezed his head into the sink, scratching at the clump of mud and rubbing the blood off his lip. He towelled off his hair and stared back at the boy in the mirror, stringy and lean with lumpy ribs.

He searched through the cupboard and found a small pair of hair-trimming clippers. Holding his fringe off his forehead, he began to cut with long, slow strokes, letting the thick clumps of hair fall down onto his feet.

Back in his room, he towelled off and got dressed. In the old Queen Anne dresser, he searched for his pocketknife, wallet, some matches, an aluminium water bottle, and a spare shirt. He found a scrap of paper and wrote a quick note.

Annie. I'll be in touch, Luke.

There was so much more he wanted to say to her, so many reasons to say *thanks* and *sorry*. But he couldn't begin to put it into words. For the moment, he hoped she would understand and not be hurt.

Luke didn't know where he would go, exactly. But he did know that he wasn't going to hang around and be assessed and re-homed like a lost dog. The only true family he had was horses, and he was going to find them, find some brumbies. Brumbies were wild and free and owned by no one.

He could go south, down to the Snowies; he knew there were plenty down there. Lawson's first horse, Dusty, had been a brumby foal from down that way, and he reckoned it was the toughest and most honest horse he had ever owned. Its feet were like iron, he said, and never needed shoeing, even for rocky ground. Brumbies had bred by natural selection in some of the toughest country in Australia.

But that cold mountain country didn't call to Luke the way outback Queensland did. Queensland had brumbies too, plenty of them. Lawson reckoned he'd seen thousands of them, roaming free in big mobs in and out of the stations. He said the station owners heli-mustered them sometimes – many of them never recovered from the long hot gallop and died days later, but the ones that did made good honest horses.

Luke threw his things into a backpack and as he went to close the dresser drawer, he saw a photo of his mother. He held the photo to his face for a moment, then placed it carefully back in the drawer. Shoving the wallet into his back pocket, he stuffed a small blanket into the pack, slung it over his shoulders and slid open the sash window.

Jess was in the mares' paddock, a curled-up figure sitting against a fence post in the dark.

'How come you're not at the wake?' Luke asked, letting himself through the gate.

She didn't answer him.

He sat down next to her and although she didn't speak, he could feel her, the warmth that flowed out of her. She was loved, loveable. She came from a different world to him. 'Sorry,' he whispered.

But still Jess didn't answer him. She sat with her arms wrapped around her knees, rocking. He could tell she was crying and he wanted to hug her, soothe her, the way he did with young horses.

Luke sat watching the black outline of a mare in the paddock, and felt suddenly exhausted. He could have lain down right there and fallen asleep under the shattered glass of the stars, with no need to talk.

Instead, he put his arms around his knees and stared up into the sky, wondering how he could have stuffed up so much in such a short time. A cloud floated away from the big silvery moon, and as though someone had pulled a cloth from over a lamp, light ran over him.

'What did you do to your face?' asked Jess suddenly.

Luke's hand flew to his cheek. It was puffy and his lip was swollen, but he was surprised that she could see it in the dark. Curse the moon. 'Umm . . .'

He couldn't bring himself to say it out loud, so he sat there in silence, feeling a wave of shame wash over him.

'Something's really wrong, isn't it? What happened? Did someone get drunk and hit you?'

'No.'

'Who did that to you?'

'I did it to myself.'

And with that, the questions stopped. She must have realised it was something bad.

'I'm taking off for a bit.'

'Where?' she asked. Her voice got squeaky. 'Where are you going? Are you coming back?'

He shrugged. 'Dunno.'

'Luke?'

'I don't know, Jessy.' It was all he could say. He wanted to sit there and pour it all out, offload it, but he didn't even know where to begin. 'I don't know what to tell you.'

'Tell me what's happened.'

'I'm not going to let them send me to another foster home.'

'What do you mean? This is your home. Harry's . . .'

Her voice faded to momentary silence as reality hit home. 'Oh, Luke . . .'

He stood up and arranged his pack on his shoulders. 'Just wanted to say bye.'

'Luke, no. Lawson wouldn't let that happen.'

Oh, yes he would. Now he would. I've stuffed up everything.

Jess's eyes ran over his face. 'Oh my God, did Lawson do that to you?'

'I told you, I did it to myself. I hit him first.'

There was a stunned silence.

'I've got to go, Jessy. I just wanted to come and say goodbye.'

She stood up and faced him. 'Shouldn't you sleep it off and decide in the morning, when you're not so upset?'

'Sleep?' He couldn't help laughing. 'I'm not good at sleeping.'

'I don't want you to go.'

Luke started walking. He felt a tremendous pulling in his gut. He had to get out of there before she convinced him to stay.

'Luke!'

He spun around. '*What?*'

She untied something from around her neck and held it out to him. 'Take my moonstone.' She shrugged. 'They're supposed to give you beautiful dreams. So Mum reckons, anyway. Never know, might help you sleep better.'

It was a pale oval-shaped stone, hung on a thin leather strap. He moved it around in his fingers and felt its smoothness.

'Promise me you'll come back,' she whispered.

He could hear the tears in her words, but he didn't answer. How could he promise her that?

'Luke?'

'I'll see you again, Jess,' he said. 'Promise.'

7

LUKE WALKED QUICKLY, cutting through the river flats and across private paddocks, trying not to think of Jess. He wanted to get to the highway before sun-up. Hunger pulled at his belly and he realised he'd barely eaten the previous day.

The sun was just beginning to show on the horizon as he made it onto the highway, and walked another kilometre or so to the truck stop. There, he bought a roadmap of Queensland, two burgers with the lot and a drink.

He sat down, unwrapped a burger and flipped the roadmap open while he crammed as much as he could into his gob.

Townsville . . . Paluma . . .

He'd heard about brumby-culling in a place called Paluma. Paluma: he'd googled it once and seen nothing but rugged dark-green mountains.

There had been a lot of slaughtering going on up that

way, too, thousands of brumbies shot from a helicopter. Looking at the terrain, Luke reckoned there'd have to be plenty still hiding. He ran his finger in a circle around the town as he bit into the second burger.

A friendly but solemn voice spoke behind him. 'That country full of *yarramin.*'

It was a voice Luke had heard before, somewhere. He looked around in surprise. A man with a dark face, neatly trimmed beard and short curly hair was staring over his shoulder at the map. He wore an orange checked shirt with short sleeves, tucked into baggy jeans that were held up with a rodeo buckle. On his head was a big black hat, beaten out of shape and scarred by harsh weather, dirt and diesel. It was the kind of hat that could tell stories of station life.

Luke realised that he had met the man before, at campdrafts. He was Lawson's mate, and often worked the yards. 'Bob, isn't it?'

'Luke,' the man nodded. He reached out a large, calloused hand to shake. 'Met you at Longwood, a while back. You rode the stallion at the funeral yesterday.'

'Yeah, that's right,' said Luke cautiously.

Bob motioned towards the seat opposite. 'Mind?'

Luke gathered up his discarded burger wrappers from the table to clear a space.

Bob cast solemn eyes over Luke's swollen face. 'Been

givin' cheek, ay,' he said, more as a statement than a question.

Luke nodded.

'And now you're taking off,' Bob concluded, pulling the cap off his water bottle and chugging it down.

Luke bit into the burger and flipped over a page in the roadmap without answering.

Bob placed the water bottle in front of him on the table and held it in both hands, turning it slowly around, as though waiting for Luke to look up and answer him.

Luke could feel his eyes on him. He turned another page.

I'm not going back.

Bob drank from the bottle again, emptying it this time. He placed it carefully back on the table and wiped his beard with his sleeve. 'I'm headed to the Gulf: plenty *yarramin* up that way too. You want a lift, you better make up your mind quick.' He screwed the cap back on the bottle and stood up. 'Blue HQ out the front. Just gotta fuel up, then I'm off.'

Luke watched Bob walk to a bin and toss the empty bottle into it before walking out the door. He stepped into a metallic blue ute and began backing it out of the parking space.

Luke quickly gathered his maps and shoved them into his pack as he scraped his chair back. The ute pulled up at a bowser, and Bob got out and began to fill the tank.

Luke reached into his back pocket for his wallet and pulled out a fifty. He held it out to Bob, who glanced at it and shook his head. 'Put that away.'

When they were on the highway, Bob put a CD into the stereo and turned it up loud enough to rule out any chance of talking, which suited Luke fine. He looked at the cover sitting on the centre console. There was a picture of some haunted-looking dude on the front.

The sun streamed in through the front window and he wished he'd bought a cheap pair of sunnies at the truck stop. The music was twangy country, similar to the stuff Lawson always played.

They've put my soul up for sale | Now there's darkness on my trail.

Luke put his head back, closed his eyes and breathed in the manky odours that seeped from the upholstery of the seats: the different people, dogs, old buckets, greasy chains, burger wrappers and leather saddles.

The CD played enough times for Luke to start to sing along to the lyrics in his head, and then they faded as sleep closed over him.

It was late afternoon when a bump in the road banged his head against the window. He woke with a jerk and realised he'd been dribbling. The same voice was still singing.

I keep on running | like a river full of pain | it keeps pulling me | dragging on my chain.

He felt something dig into his hip and pulled the moonstone out of his pocket. It was milky and shiny, with faint colours reflecting off it. He untangled the leather strap, pulled it over his head and tucked the stone safely under his shirt, then fell asleep again.

When he woke it was evening and the same voice was still singing.

They're watching me now | The cockies on the rail | The hammer's coming down | My soul is up for sale.

Bob sang along loudly as he pulled over into a truck stop, rolled up next to a petrol bowser and wrenched on the handbrake.

Luke got out and stretched his legs. A warm gust of air hit him in the face, bringing with it familiar sounds and smells of the night: mulga trees and red earth, dry air, mixed with petrol and oil, tyres on a distant freeway, screeching bats and country music floating out of overhead speakers.

He went into the roadhouse and ordered two steak sandwiches. While he was waiting for them to cook, he wandered over to the small grocery section.

The first thing he noticed was some bundles of fresh asparagus. Jess's family had an organic farm where they grew asparagus and other small crops; she used to bring bunches of it over to Harry's place on the weekends. She reckoned it made you live forever. When Jess had found out Harry had lung cancer, she'd started bringing it around by the boxful, convinced it would save his life – packed with vitamin C, it was. Harry always sneaked the asparagus onto Luke's plate while she wasn't looking, which he didn't mind as long as it wasn't all soggy.

Luke took two bunches lest he end up a wheezing old man attached to oxygen bottles. Then he grabbed a budget box of muesli bars and a net bag of apples.

Outside, Bob was already getting back into the ute.

'Where are we going?' asked Luke, climbing in and pulling the seatbelt over his lap. He pulled out an asparagus spear and chewed on it, then began to unwrap his sandwiches.

'Mount Isa first, then I've gotta catch up with some brothers up in the Gulf,' said Bob, 'then a station out there's got some work for me.' He screwed up his nose. 'What's that green stuff?'

'Asparagus. So I'll live forever.' He held them out to Bob. 'Want one?'

Bob eyed the green spears suspiciously. 'I don't wanna live forever.'

Luke shrugged. 'What's in the Gulf?'

'Big river full of fish,' said Bob, leaning in front of Luke and opening the glovebox. He placed in it something lumpy, wrapped in foil. 'You like fishing?'

'What was that?'

'Bait,' said Bob, starting the engine.

'Never been fishing.'

'You haven't lived!'

8

AN EXPLOSIVE BANG came from the back of the car and it swerved violently to one side. Bob swore loudly as he fought with the steering wheel.

'Blowout,' he said, guiding the ute to the edge of the road. Each time he touched the brake, the ute pulled heavily into the middle of the highway. Bob let it roll to a stop, pulled on the handbrake and opened the door. He got out and cursed again when he saw the damage.

Luke walked around to the driver's side. The back tyre was in shreds. 'Got a spare?'

'Yeah,' said Bob, unclipping the big tarp off the back and throwing it aside.

'Need a hand?'

'Nah, won't take long.'

'I'm gonna see a man about a dog,' said Luke, looking for a good clump of bushes in the scrub along the side of the road. He spotted some small trees in the distance and began wading through scratchy golden grass and small prickly shrubs.

He hadn't gone far when there was a sudden burst of activity right in front of him. A small red horse sprang out of the grass and Luke jumped back in surprise. The horse slowed to an agonised hobble on three legs. It was terribly thin and scrambled along with its head lowered, ears flicking around and nostrils flared.

'Hey, you poor fella,' said Luke. 'What have you done to yourself?'

He stood quietly, not wanting to force the horse on further, and looked it over for brands. There were none.

'You got a home to go to?' he asked softly, squatting and making himself smaller. He folded his arms across his chest. The horse seemed to relax a little and, encouraged, Luke turned his eyes away from it. 'I'm not gonna hurt you.'

The horse closed its eyes and screwed up its nose, clearly in pain. Luke tried to see its hoof but it was obscured by grass. He kept his eyes focused well ahead of the horse and crept closer, talking softly. It shuffled a couple more steps forward. Luke raised himself up and got a better look at its leg. He couldn't see any swelling. It must be in the hoof.

Luke took note of where the horse stood and then

turned his back on it, stepping slowly and carefully backwards, closer to the animal. He listened for any movements but heard none until he was close enough to hear it breathing: short, raspy, suspicious breaths. But it didn't move away from him.

He slowly crouched down and knelt on one knee. He felt a warm puff of grassy breath on his neck and smiled. 'Hey, fella.'

Rubbery lips nibbled at his hair.

Luke turned his head and saw a coppery nose from the corner of his eye. He extended the back of his hand and touched the horse's leg.

The horse stiffened but stood quiet. Luke rubbed the back of his hand up and down the hard bony part of its leg, then down to the hoof. It was held above the ground, trembling. Something sharp was wedged into the sole of its foot.

'Geez, this is no place to be getting a puncture wound, Red,' he said to the horse. 'You want some help getting that out?'

Luke reached into his back pocket for his knife and flicked it open. 'You're gonna have to stand still for me,' he said, sliding the blade down the side of the glass chunk, into the horny white sole. The hoof itself was in good condition, perfectly shaped with a thick wall and no signs of bruising, despite the rough country.

'If I can get that glass out and it hasn't gone down to the bone, I reckon that foot might heal okay.'

He dug carefully around the glass and flicked it out onto the stones. Fresh red blood trickled out of the wound.

'That's not a good sign, Red, but you've got pretty tough feet and there's no heat in your leg, so who knows, you might just heal.' He stood up slowly and saw Bob back at the ute, watching him. Luke grinned.

Bob scowled in response and lowered himself into the ute.

'I better be going, Red,' said Luke. 'Don't wanna miss my ride.' He turned slowly to the horse and ran the back of his hand over its shoulder, which was flat and tri-angular with no spare flesh.

The horse lifted its head and snorted. It nipped cheekily at Luke's face and sprang away from him, cantering on four legs, instantly free of pain. Luke watched it run for a bit and then disappear into a grove of trees.

He ran back to the ute, and jumped into the front seat just as it began to roll onto the highway.

'He had a bit of glass in his foot,' said Luke, slamming the door and reaching for his belt. 'Reckon he's off one of the stations? He's in pretty bad nick.'

'That's no station horse,' said Bob, flicking on the indicator and pulling out onto the road. He put on his sunglasses, turned the stereo up and stared straight ahead, accelerating towards the next town and into a burning sunset.

Luke stared at him. He could see a frown above the man's sunnies. 'What's wrong?'

Bob took a while to answer him. 'Nothin'.'

'It was in pain. I couldn't just leave it.'

Bob shrugged. 'Just never seen a brumby trust a human like that before.'

'It was probably a station horse.'

Bob shook his head. 'Nup.'

Bob drove without talking and Luke ate his steak sandwiches, wondering how long he would be able to afford to eat so well. He needed money. He needed a job.

His phone suddenly began trumpeting the arrival of a text message. He reached between his knees and pulled it out of his pack. It was from Lawson. Lawson hardly ever texted; his fingers were too big. Luke felt a sharp sting in his chest.

Telling me to rack off and don't come back.

He flipped the phone shut and sat there staring out the window at the big flat fields rolling past. The sun was setting down low and a pale haze of pink and gold glowed above the horizon. The phone was in his hand with the message that would cut him off from his family for good. He gritted his teeth and opened it again.

The phone beeped at him, out of charge. He quickly thumbed around for the read button, but the screen faded before his eyes.

'I hate that!' Luke smacked the phone hard against the dashboard. 'What sort of phone have you got?' he asked Bob, hoping he might be able to switch batteries.

Bob looked at him blankly.

Luke hurled the comatose phone out the window.

Bob raised an eyebrow and drove on, whistling quietly to his CD.

They kept driving, through the night and into the next day. Bob pulled over every now and then for a power-kip, and then drove on. As the second day slipped into night, a mass of lights appeared in front of them. Directly ahead were two tall smoke stacks, lit up like a big cruise ship.

'Welcome to the Isa,' Bob announced wearily.

'What is that thing?' asked Luke.

'A mine,' said Bob. 'This country is full of minerals: copper, lead, silver, zinc.' He pulled away from a set of traffic lights, drove until they were on the other side of the city limits and then pulled over. 'Stop and have a kip, ay. I'm beat.' He rolled out his swag in the back of the ute and left Luke to stretch out across the bench seat in the front.

Luke didn't know or care what time of night it was or where the hell they'd ended up. He just needed to lie down. He kicked his boots off and let the waft of stinky socks curl around the inside of the cabin. He pulled the moonstone out from under his shirt.

It's supposed to give you beautiful dreams.

It didn't work. The night passed unevenly, in lurches and dragging lulls. He tossed restlessly about inside the cabin, occasionally drifting off and being woken again by the roar and rattle of a truck barrelling along the highway. In the moments that he lay awake, he thought of Lawson, standing in the stable doorway, his hard, impassive voice.

You wanna be a Blake, you gotta earn the name.

When he drifted off, he was haunted by Bob's music.

The hammer's coming down.

Faceless soldiers, dark shapes, footfalls hammering against his skull.

Then he would wake again and think of Jess, her carefree laughter and the touch of her hand on his arm, and it would soothe him. He held the moonstone again and begged it for sleep. Eventually it worked.

Until Bob yanked the car door open, pulling the arm rest out from under his head. 'Morning.'

Luke groaned. 'I'm wrecked,' he mumbled. His body

was wet with sweat and his mouth tasted as if it had been stuck together with glue. The inside of the cabin was stuffy and airless. Outside was dry and hot, with not a breath of wind.

'Get some stuff in town and get out of here, ay?' said Bob, climbing in and starting the engine. He had already had a splash with water and wet his hair down.

'Is there a river around here?' asked Luke, ungluing his mouth to speak and scratching at his head.

'Yeah, just up the road,' said Bob, sticking the ute into gear and accelerating back towards town. 'Get some shopping first.'

9

AFTER ANOTHER WHOLE DAY of driving, bumping along a narrow track of cracked brown earth, Bob took a sudden left-hand turn. Within seconds, Luke was staring at a lush oasis. The track dipped down onto a low causeway, crossed by a crystal-clear stream with tall paperbark trees, strappy pandanus and fan palms lining its banks. The sound of rushing water and twittering birds offered a sanctuary from the blistering heat. Beyond the causeway, tucked in behind a bend in the river, was a twin-cab ute. A blue plume of smoke wafted lazily nearby.

'Stop here, ay?' said Bob, killing the engine. He stepped out of the car and pushed up his sunglasses, then cupped his hands over his mouth and called, 'Hey!'

On the opposite bank, a man's voice came back. 'Hey! Over 'ere.'

Bob kicked off his thongs and began rolling up his jeans. 'Coming?' he said to Luke.

Luke didn't bother rolling his up. It was so hot he welcomed the idea of cold wet jeans. He followed Bob in and waded through the knee-deep water. It was cool and slow-moving. The concrete causeway was green with moss and slippery under his feet. 'What river's this?'

'The Rubicon, boy,' said Bob. 'You're crossing the Rubicon.'

A man with wild, springy black hair and an untrimmed beard, wearing just an old pair of footy shorts, waded through the water. 'The turtles are comin' down the river,' he called out, holding his hands out to the size of a football. 'Saw two of 'em. Big fat ones.'

'How big?' chuckled Bob.

'They were *huge*, brother, big dinosaur ones. Tex saw 'em.' He called over his shoulder, 'Didn't you, Tex?'

Luke heard a confused mumbling as someone came sloshing around the bend.

'Them turtles, Tex,' the man reiterated. 'Huge, weren't they?'

An older man with long skinny black legs and silvery hair waded towards them. In his hand, he clasped a small turtle by the neck. Its shell was barely larger than the man's fist. 'Oh yeah, they were huge.' He held the turtle up and grinned. 'This one's just a little baby one. Mum and Dad got away.'

'You're not gonna eat that poor thing?' said Bob.

Tex looked at it and pursed his lips. 'Bit scrawny, ay.' He flipped it back into the river.

'You stop at the shop?' asked the wild-haired one.

'Yeah,' drawled Bob. 'Just got the usual roadside crap.'

Luke stepped out from behind Bob. 'Oh yeah, and I brought a young fulla too. This is Luke.'

Luke felt two pairs of shrewd eyes run over him. The mood changed immediately.

The man with the springy hair stepped up onto the bank. He was big, with heavy features, but his movements were smooth and liquid, almost like a cat's.

'Tyson,' he said, shaking Luke's hand, first in the way Luke was accustomed to and then urban-style, rotating his palm to take Luke's thumb in a fist-like hold. His grip was strong but cordial, and his skin felt smooth, almost papery.

'Tyson,' Luke nodded.

The man called Tex was slower to come over. He held out a long, sinewy arm and offered a hand full of bumpy knuckles. 'Tex,' he said, in a voice that went with his posture: easy, gentle and welcoming. He seemed senior to the other two men, and not just because of his age; he moved and spoke with authority. 'How are ya, Luke?' he asked.

'Yeah, good,' answered Luke. And he meant it. Something about the place was indescribably peaceful and he felt lucky to be standing there. He had no idea how long he was going to be around or what he would be doing with himself, but he didn't care. The place seemed special, ancient and untouched, as though a dinosaur could come clumping through the trees at any moment. If he had to be homeless, this was a heck of a nice place to do it.

The men began talking among themselves, with words and names that Luke didn't know. They spoke quickly, in voices too accented for him to understand. Luke stood there awkwardly, not sure what to do with himself. He picked up the word *yarramin*, which he knew meant 'horse', and wondered if they were talking about him.

Tyson squatted next to the fire as he talked, feeding the small pile of coals. He waved a finger at the ground, indicating that Luke should sit down, and he did as was suggested. Bob plonked a bag of groceries on the ground and sat next to him. Luke turned to him. 'What did you just say to them?'

'What do you mean?' asked Bob.

'Just then, you were talking about me. What did you say?'

'I told them you were good with horses, wanted to come and see some wild brumbies.'

He had said more than that, Luke was sure, but he was okay with that as a general introduction.

Tyson pulled out a can of food from Bob's shopping

bag. 'Baked beans? What, am I a vegetarian now?'

'For breakfast,' said Bob. 'Thought you fullas were getting some wild meat. Didn't know all you could catch was a puny little turtle.'

Tyson ignored him and kept rummaging. 'Hmm, yams.' He poked them into the coals with a stick. 'So you're a bit of a fighter, ay, Luke?' he said.

Luke ran a thumb over his lip. 'Guess I must be.'

'And you're looking for brumbies, ay?'

'I wouldn't mind gentling one,' said Luke. 'A real one, out in the wild, not in a yard. I reckon taming a brumby would be really cool.'

'You won't have any trouble finding them around here,' said Tyson.

'Like horses, hey?' asked Tex, joining them.

'Yeah,' said Luke. 'Horses go way back in my family. I lost my first one, but my second family are riders too. My brother reckons the horses up here have got really hard feet. He's a farrier.'

Tyson began rummaging through the bag again. 'No sauce?'

'What, you think it's Christmas or something?' said Bob. 'Anyway, that stuff's full of sugar.'

'Last time *you* go to the shop,' Tyson grumbled back. He pulled a packet out of the bag. 'Noodles,' he grunted with contempt. 'Bring a can opener, or a *pot*?'

73

Bob groaned in annoyance.

Tyson stuffed everything back in the plastic bag. 'I'm not eating any of that crap,' he grumbled. He folded his arms across his chest. 'Gonna have to do some serious fishing.'

'So you ride them horses too?' asked Tex from the other side of the fire.

'Yep,' Luke answered. 'I've been doing a few camp-drafts.'

The other men didn't pursue the conversation. They began talking quietly in their own language again. They seemed to be disagreeing about something. As Luke sat on the outer, the image of Lawson standing over him with blood on his lip came flashing into his memory, and it made him feel sick that he'd hit him.

'Me and Lawson had a bit of a falling out,' he blurted for no particular reason. 'I wish I could take him a brumby home. He'd love it.' He paused and then said quietly, 'Make it up to him.'

The campsite was quiet for a while longer until Tyson spoke. 'That's good thinking, Luke.'

Luke felt a surprising wave of relief at the approval in Tyson's voice.

Tex picked up a stick and began scraping at a mound of coals, revealing a lump wrapped in foil, sitting in a shallow hole. A waft of cooked meat hit Luke in the nose.

'Is that kangaroo?' he asked.

Tyson and Bob both laughed.

'I got us a big barra,' said Tyson. He turned to Bob. 'You wanna teach this poor kid to fish while he's here, bro.'

The fish was like nothing Luke had ever tasted before; juicy white slabs of meat, infused with a smoky flavour from the coals and drizzled with bush limes that Tex had collected at a property on his way to the river. The yams were good too: fluffy and sweet on the inside, charcoal on the outside, which was okay if he dusted the gritty bits off.

As he talked to the men that night, Luke found out that Tex did the mail run every Saturday, out to all the stations in the lower Gulf. After his deliveries he often stayed to fish in the river. Tyson was some sort of advisor to the government, something to do with education, and that got him travelling around too. This wasn't their country. They were all from further down south, but the fishing was better up here.

Later, Tex and Tyson rolled out swags and fell asleep by the fire. Luke unrolled his blanket and threw it around his shoulders. As he watched the flames lap at a large chunk of log, he turned to Bob. 'How come Tex was asking me about the horses like that?'

'Ah yeah, that,' said Bob, seemingly mesmerised by

the fire. 'Tex is wary about people with horse dreaming.'

'Horse dreaming?'

'Yeah, you got big horse dream kicking around inside you, boy,' said Bob. 'The way you walk with 'em like that—' He shook his head. '—it's not normal. Tex's worried about *purri purri* – black magic.'

'*Purri purri?* I thought you fellas were good horsemen too. Harry reckoned Aboriginal stockmen were the best around,' said Luke. 'Like you.'

'Yeah, there are big traditions around Aboriginal stockmen, but also big fear of horses, mostly with the older fellas, a lot of lore about them carrying devils in their bellies, being sorcerers or demons, spirits in disguise. Old clever fellas run with 'em, do terrible things.'

Bob went quiet for a moment. His face, lit by the glow of the fire, was still. 'It goes back to first contact, back to the massacres. The stories were told to keep the kids away from bad places.'

Luke stared into the fire. It made him feel uncomfortable, sitting there imagining what his ancestors might have done to Bob's.

'My people have a lot of sad stories, Luke. Tex'll be all right once he works out you're not playing with magic.' Bob got up and stretched his legs.

Luke lay back with his blanket wrapped around his shoulders and gazed up at the stars. Locusts hovered in the light over the fire and he could hear cane toads crashing about in the shrubs and grasses around him. The trees were tall and scrawny without much cover.

He tried to close his eyes and sleep but his brain kept replaying the fight with Lawson, bringing a surge of shame each time, taking him back to a place that Harry had once pulled him out of.

After lying there for half an eternity, trying to deflect the sadness with thoughts of wild brumbies, he decided to get up and go for a wander. He walked out beyond the river into a paddock. The moon was rising, full and beautiful, turning the soft darkness of the land into tangles of black and silver. Although unsure of the ground beneath him, Luke set off at a slow jog, aiming for a small range of hills.

He ran down a little gully and over a stream. On the other side, the long grass swished as he brushed through it. He settled into a steady rhythm and as he began to pant he felt better, so he pushed it out a bit harder, blowing heavier and heavier with every mile he chewed up. It took longer than he expected to get to the line of hills. It seemed that the more he ran towards them, the further away they got, as though they were leading him on a chase. A fence loomed. He grabbed a post and vaulted over to the next paddock.

There, he saw silhouettes of horses, heads raised, ears alert, ready to flee. Luke slowed to a walk, then stopped and bent over with his hands on his knees, waiting for his breath to slow. A couple of mares ushered their foals away. The other horses resumed grazing.

Luke quietly approached what looked like an old quarter horse and ran his hand down its shoulder. He felt the broken pelt of a hot brand on its shoulder and wondered what sort of life the horse had had. Had it mustered cattle or been a campdrafting star? Been an old schoolmaster for the kids? He was a gentle old soul, this one. Luke ran his hands over the horse's neck, put his face against it, breathed in its scent, and felt the tension ease from his body.

The salty smell of horse sweat brought back images of home: of Legs and all the horses; Harry, limping down the stable aisle and sneaking a fag when he thought no one else was around; the warm sunny days spent training horses, sweeping out feedrooms and unloading trucks of lucerne. He remembered all the laughter and knocking about with Tom, hanging out at the mares' paddock with Jess, watching the foals play.

That life never belonged to me, anyway.

The old quarter horse put his head down to graze.

Luke took a handful of mane and slipped up onto his back. It was broad and as comfy as a couch. He lay along it with his chest over the horse's wither, hung an arm either side of his shoulders and clasped his feet together over the rump. The old horse snorted softly and kept grazing. Luke closed his eyes and let his head empty completely, until only the in and out of his breath ran gently through his conscience, interspersed with the slow pull and munch of the horse grazing. The past and the future ceased to exist. He was in the here and now, filled with peace and comfort.

But as he lay there, the beat of the horse's heart became gradually louder. It began to pound and hammer like a drum. The music from Bob's car, the same voice, boomed into his head.

The hammer's coming down | The hammer's coming down | Who's gonna buy my soul?

A horse screamed in the distance but it was muted, muffled by rocky hills and scrubs. There was something strange about it. Luke thought briefly about getting up and searching for it, but his body was heavy, so heavy. He lay along the horse's back, motionless except for the slow rise and fall of his breath. The screaming stopped and he drifted away again.

Sometime later a cool breeze woke him. He wasn't sure if he had really fallen asleep or if he had just drifted into a kind of trance. The horse walked and grazed, walked and grazed, and he rolled with the movement of its body as though on a boat.

Then he heard the horse again, a haunting, screaming noise so far away that it seemed to come from another time and place. It ripped through his soul like icy wind. There was another tiny, indefinable noise – a cry perhaps, or a bleat.

10

WHEN HE WOKE he found himself lying in a field. It was morning and the sun cast its warmth over him. He could see nothing but grey-golden grass all around him. It was hot and birds tweeted in the new day. A nearby horse blew the dust from its nostrils.

Luke wandered back to the camp and marvelled at the dramatic colour of the river. It was a pale icy blue, unlike any river he'd seen. Weeping branches hung over it, resting their fingertips in the slow-moving water, and knotted tree roots curled from its mossy banks like gnarly old toes over a step.

At the campsite, the fire had died down to a pile of ash. Next to it, Tyson was hacking at a tin of baked beans with a pocket knife.

'This is gonna *wreck* my knife,' he said.

Luke pulled the budget box of muesli bars from his pack and chucked them over to him.

'Hmm, horse food,' Tyson said, turning the box over and reading the label. 'Got anything else?'

Luke rummaged around in his pack for the net bag of apples. 'Don't bruise them.'

'More horse food,' said Tyson, but he took one out anyway. He bit it clean in two and chewed noisily.

Luke pulled his knife out of his pocket and resumed opening the baked beans.

'You know, there are three kinds of men in the world, Luke,' said Tyson, lying back, looking up at the sky and speaking through his apple. 'Fighters, soldiers and warriors. You know the difference?'

Luke ran a hand over his cheek. It felt slightly swollen and he guessed there was still bruising. 'I know what a fighter is.'

'Yeah, I can see that,' said Tyson.

'Fighting makes me feel good sometimes,' Luke admitted. 'Powerful.'

Tyson snorted. 'That's a false power,' he said. 'Didn't do you much good with your brother, did it?'

Luke bristled. 'What would you know about Lawson?'

'Probably more than you think, young fulla. You're not the Lone Ranger when it comes to all that stuff.' Tyson sat up, pulled a muesli bar from the box, unwrapped it and began chewing. 'Anyway, then there's soldiers,' he said. 'Soldiers do what they're told, even if it's wrong. They have strict rules in their work, but not in their lives, and this makes problems too.'

He screwed the wrapper up in his hand and tossed it into the coals. 'Today you young fullas wanna carry on like warriors, but you've got no code,' he said. 'I can tell you now, it's not the fighting that makes you feel good, Luke.' Tyson paused and wiped his mouth with a sleeve. 'It's the violence.'

He pointed half a muesli bar at Luke. 'Me, I love a bit of violence. But it's gotta have some rules. If you don't have rules, you just end up a criminal. You end up in prison.'

'Lawson *broke* the rules,' said Luke coldly. 'I was fine until he broke the rules.'

'What rules?' asked Tyson. 'You tell me what rules he broke.'

'He got in my face at the wrong time,' said Luke flatly. He didn't need to give this guy any more information than that. It was none of his business.

'That's bull,' said Tyson. 'You were totally out of control.' He sprang to his feet in a sudden, swift movement and stood in front of Luke. 'Here, get up,' he said, gesturing at him with an arm. 'Get up and show me that knife.' He pulled his T-shirt over his head and tossed it on the ground. Then he pulled his knife from a back pocket, flicked it open and held it in front of him.

Luke shrank back, dumbfounded.

'Come on, powerful boy,' Tyson taunted. 'Let's see what rules you fight by!'

Luke put up his hands in a gesture of peace. 'I don't want to get into a fight with you.'

'Come on,' said Tyson in a more friendly tone. 'Violence can be good. I'll show you.'

'It's all right, I believe you,' said Luke. There was no way he was getting up and going face-to-face with that man and that knife. Tyson was tall and probably fairly fit, although he might have eaten a few too many muesli bars in his time.

Tyson rolled his eyes. 'Comahhhn, I'll take it easy on you. Get up!'

Intrigued, Luke stood up.

Tyson waved a hand towards himself. 'Knife.'

Luke pulled it from his pocket and held it out to Tyson.

Tyson shook his head. 'Open it.'

'What for?'

'Trust me.'

'I don't know you from a bar of soap, mate,' said Luke, ready to walk away. He was no stranger to violence, but not with big hairy blokes like Tyson, and not with knives. 'That's dirty fighting.'

'Nah, this is a good knife-fighting way,' Tyson continued, unperturbed. 'It came from the fullas down south, you'll love it.' He set his feet apart and held his knife up. 'We can only cut and stab each other on the arms or the back, okay.'

Luke took another step back. 'You're not serious?'

'It's okay,' Tyson assured him. 'It's hard to land a shot if you follow the rules.' He grinned. 'That's if you follow the rules. And there's a twist. We'll get Tex to check out our wounds at the end and he can say the winner, and then whoever that is, he gets cut up same as the loser.' He was beaming. It was obvious he loved this stuff.

Luke just stared at him.

'It's pretty cool, ay?' said Tyson. 'If I get you a good one, you get to cut me back. That way no one can walk away with a grudge.'

'What makes you think *you* would get *me*?' asked Luke, feeling himself being sucked into the challenge. 'You might be three times the size of me, but that doesn't mean you're quick.'

Tyson chuckled and switched his knife from hand to hand. He eyeballed Luke's knife. 'You gonna open that thing?'

At that moment, a deep, gentle voice spoke behind him. 'Put that away, Luke.'

Luke spun around and saw Tex holding out two thick black textas. 'This is how we do it these days. Tyson's just playing with you.'

Luke ran his eyes from Tex to Tyson, who stood there grinning, challenging. It irritated the hell out of him.

There were no evident scars on Tyson's body, and Luke wondered whether he was really good at this game or really bad at it, or maybe he had never really done it with knives before. But then he hadn't seen Tyson's back. He began circling, hoping to catch a glimpse of it. Tyson moved against him, denying him the chance to find out.

Luke lifted his shirt up over his head and threw it on the ground. Tyson's eyes ran over his torso and Luke spotted the fleeting look of shock that most people got when they saw his ribs. 'I've taken on bigger than you before,' said Luke, not taking his eyes off Tyson.

'And come off second best,' noted Tyson, his expression noticeably different from moments before.

Luke pulled his knife blade out of its handle. 'You don't know that.'

Tex's hand wrapped around his wrist. 'You don't need to do that, boy.'

'Yeah, I do,' said Luke, without taking his eyes off Tyson. He shook off Tex's hand, and continued to step cautiously around the big man. Then without hesitating, he lashed out and swiped hard across Tyson's left shoulder.

The knife was blunt, but it left a mark all the same, and a trickle of blood dribbled down into the man's armpit.

Tyson barely moved, but his eyes blazed suddenly with anger. He crouched, as if ready to pounce and a menacing, don't-mess-with-me look came over his face.

Luke's felt a sudden surge of confidence. 'C'mahhhn, I'll take it easy on you,' he teased, mimicking Tyson's earlier words.

'Cocky,' noted Tyson, stepping carefully around, eyes on Luke.

There were other voices, Tex's and Bob's, but Luke didn't listen. He couldn't take his eyes off Tyson. He had started something.

Luke lunged, hoping to surprise him again. Tyson lifted an arm, nearly dislocating Luke's elbow, then came around behind him with the other hand and slashed lightly across his back.

The stroke left a scorching line of cold and, although it didn't feel deep, it was enough to make Luke's anger boil. He wanted to hurt Tyson this time, cut him real good, but something stopped him: the same something that steadied Tyson's stroke and kept it in check. Luke would have to wear the same scar, bear the same injury. By hurting Tyson, he would be hurting himself.

It added a new element to the fight, that was for sure: self-control, which Luke had never been able to master.

When he fought, he was usually just lost in a haze of anger. But unless he wanted to end up in pieces, he'd have to master that quickly. He breathed a few deep breaths, and as he did so, Tyson danced to the side and swung his knife again.

Luke jumped backwards, retreating into bushes. His bare feet landed on sharp sticks and spiky leaves. He stumbled, then crashed onto his back with a heavy thud.

Tyson looked down at him. 'You get the idea now?'

Luke snarled and snapped his knife shut. He tossed it at Tyson, who snatched it out of the air and extended a hand to help him up.

Luke pushed the hand away. 'Whatever.'

As he picked himself up off the ground, Tyson slapped him on the back and Luke swung at him. He wasn't ready to make nice just yet, he was still pumped with adrenaline and anger.

Tyson ducked easily and held out Luke's knife. 'Want another go, my friend?'

Luke walked past him without speaking.

Over by the ute, Tex took Luke by the shoulders and turned him about, inspecting his back.

'Is it bad?' asked Luke, twisting to look over his shoulder.

'Is what bad?' asked Tex. He pushed Luke away, finished with him for the moment, and walked over to Tyson.

Tex smacked the man on the back of the head with an open hand and growled something at him. Tyson mumbled back and Tex whacked him again. He grabbed Tyson's arm and ran a thumb along the small cut on his shoulder.

'Am I s'posed to go cut a little white fulla now?' he said, clearly agitated.

Little white fulla? Luke walked over and handed Tex the knife, staring him straight in the eye. 'It's my cut, I earned it,' he said, turning to present his shoulder. 'And what about him?' Luke gestured towards Tyson. 'Doesn't he get a cut on his back?'

The faintest smile slipped across Tyson's face and Luke caught an answering flash of humour in Tex's eyes. Tyson handed his knife to the older man and presented his back.

Tex took the knife and slowly ran the flat back edge of the blade across Tyson's back, leaving not a trace of a cut. He turned to Luke. 'Happy?'

'What?' Luke twisted his body, trying to glance over his shoulder at the site of Tyson's hit. 'Didn't he even cut me?'

Luke didn't know whether to be grateful or severely insulted. He straightened up and glared at Tyson. 'You reckon I'm soft or something?'

He turned his shoulder to Tex again and held out his knife. 'I earned it.'

'Okay, Luke. Come and sit by the fire,' said Tex, opening Luke's knife and walking to the pile of ashes. Luke followed him and sat cross-legged where Tex pointed.

'It's important you realise this is only done at the right time, in the right place and in the right company,' Tex said. He glared at Tyson. 'You're open to the spirits now.'

Tex glanced at Tyson's upper arm once more and then swiftly slashed Luke's shoulder. Luke clamped his teeth together against the searing pain as blood trickled warmly down his arm. It felt strangely good.

Tex bent to pick up a handful of ashes.

'Is that to make it like an initiation scar?' asked Luke.

Tex scoffed. 'It's so tiny. Don't want it to heal away and you forget the lesson it taught you.' He smeared the ashes through the cut.

Tex picked up another handful of ashes and gestured for Tyson to come over. 'You don't forget this lesson either!'

Bob interjected something in his own language from the sidelines, causing the other two men to snigger.

'What?' Luke demanded.

Tex flicked open the knife again and looked down at Luke's crotch with a wicked glint in his eye. 'Bob says we should initiate you properly.'

Luke gasped and grabbed his crotch. 'Umm, somebody already beat you to it,' he said, feeling grateful to his parents for the first time in his life.

The men disintegrated into peals of laughter.

That night Luke wrapped his blanket around his shoulders and curled up next to the fire to sleep. The night sky was thick with clouds, bringing a darkness over the river crossing that felt strangely claustrophobic and unnatural. Beyond the glowing coals he could hear the sounds of the river – the *plip* of a fish as it jumped at an insect, water running over tree roots – but he couldn't see it. The darkness built walls around him, making him toss about restlessly.

He ran a hand over the scar on his arm and the gentle pain somehow brought order to his mind.

Rules, there's got to be rules, a code.

He pulled the moonstone out from under his shirt and glanced down at it. It took on new colours from the glow of the fire, as though the flames had leapt into it and come to life. He moved it around slowly in his hand, watching the colours flash and change. It was beautiful, alive and sparkling, like Jess.

He laughed quietly to himself as he thought of her clambering around on the back of Legsy, hanging off the side and laughing like an idiot, waving madly across the valley. *'Dad's slashing the paddock, look!'*

He wished he could climb to the top of a nearby mountain, look out across the country and find her. If he could, he would wave madly and yell, 'Hi, Jessy!'

But he couldn't. He had crossed the point of no return, crossed the Rubicon, like Bob had said. Perhaps one day he would run into her again, at a campdraft, or an ag show.

Then he laughed at himself. What campdrafts? The horses were never his. They were gone.

11

IT WAS BARELY MORNING. The air was still and the sky was beginning to change colour to the east, silhouetting the low hills. The distant scream of a horse rang in his ears, unsettling him.

He rose, stretched, and headed out towards the grassland, away from the river. Out in the open savannah he stood and gazed at the billions of stars, glittering against the fading blue velvet. He could clearly see the Saucepan and the Seven Sisters. Between them was another constellation that looked a bit like a man. The rest, the smaller ones, were being pulled back into the cosmos to wait for another night.

Luke began to walk. The exercise felt good and before long he was jogging, the steady thump of his feet matching the beat from his dreams, lifting his arms above the long grass as he swished through. By the time he got to the foot of the hills he was drenched with sweat and gasping for breath.

He made his way upward and the country around him changed again, from dry, golden grass to grey-green mounds of needle-tipped spinifex with occasional shrubs and small trees. His boots crunched over the stones.

A terrible scream made him stop in his tracks. It was real this time. No dream or ghost, not a nightmare; somewhere, there was a very real and very distressed horse. There was another sound, like a branch being shaken but more . . . metallic. It jangled erratically and then was silent.

Luke stopped and listened: nothing but twittering birds, whirring insects and the sound of his own lungs, panting.

He began walking again, stepping carefully around the spinifex.

There was a throaty, wheezing noise and then another rustling for a few seconds. Luke stopped. An exhausted groan, more rustling and a thud.

He knew the sound. It was a horse, fighting against wire. But where? Out here? Tyson had said there were brumbies. He looked around. The country was rough, a sea of jagged red rocks, no matter which way he looked. A dry, hot wind blew.

Then he saw it: a makeshift yard. A trap.

It was barely visible behind stunted shrubs and scrawny trees and it was only because the horizontal branches of the gate were out of place that he even spotted it. Barbed wire gleamed silvery new in the sunlight. It ran about four feet high and looped around some saplings. Hand-sawn tree branches had been wired up to form an arrow-shaped gate, designed to let something in but not out.

Luke walked closer, homing his sights in on the scene. There was another explosion of movement and he saw the bony curve of a horse's back rise above the spinifex and wire. It thrashed wildly and then disappeared with another groan and a thud.

His first instinct was to run and help it, untangle it. He wanted to hold it still and calm it so it didn't hurt itself any more. But it was a wild animal, it would be terrified of him.

He stopped and squatted low, making himself invisible. There was a rustling sound beside him and he turned to see a shape disappear behind a clump of rocks. A dingo, perhaps? He crept forwards on his hands and knees for some way to get a good look at the horse. Like an insect caught in a huge spiderweb, a mare lay on its side, her head and two front legs tangled in wire.

It was a sickening sight. A whole ear hung by a flap of skin off the side of the animal's head and one eye was a mass of dried blood. Her two front legs were stripped of flesh, down to the bone. There were flies all over her. She must have been stuck there for days.

Luke felt for the pocketknife in his back pocket. It had a tiny pair of pliers, but they were laughably small. No way would they cut through barbed wire. He felt sick when he realised that there was only one way he could help her.

I can't.

There was a tiny sound, a bleating, not far off. A goat or a lamb? He spun around, and again caught a glimpse of red disappearing behind some low shrubs. His heart sank as he realised it must be a foal. It was small too, and probably wouldn't survive without its mother. Dingoes would get it.

He pulled his T-shirt off and bunched it up. With his other hand he flicked open his knife. He hesitated for just a moment longer, then approached the mare.

I have to.

He ran the last couple of steps and threw himself on her neck, holding her down with his knee while he threw the T-shirt over her eyes. She struggled wildly and the barbed wire around her head slashed across Luke's hand. He tried to ignore the pain. Once he had her eyes covered and sat on her neck, she lay quiet, but her breath still blew in terrified snorts from her nostrils.

She struggled only briefly when he cut the jugular, but the sound was terrible, gurgling and choking. Had he cut something wrong? – the windpipe? 'Oh God, I'm sorry, I'm so sorry,' he sobbed.

As her struggles slowed, Luke brought his shoulder up to his face and wiped away the sweat and tears.

He looked around for the foal and spotted the flick of its tail fifty metres or so away. Its pale orange coat blended perfectly into the landscape, making it hard to believe that the brumbies didn't really belong there, that they were a feral pest that people trapped and killed.

The foal trotted a few steps and stopped again, nickering anxiously.

'Yeah, sucks big time, doesn't it,' he said to it. 'Same thing happened to me.'

He got up and wiped his hands across the back of his jeans without thinking, then looked down and saw his bloodsoaked shirt over the face of the mare. He stooped down and picked it up. His jeans were also soaked in blood. It was everywhere – gallons of the stuff, oozing over the ground like warm syrup. The flies were all over it. He looked at the lifeless lump, still coiled in wire, and curled his lip. What a lousy thing to do to an animal.

'Now who's gonna look after you?' he said to the foal, which still paced about on the perimeters, nickering.

He walked to the hand-sawn gate and pulled at it. He kicked at it and twisted it until it lay in a mangled heap. Not that he needed to; the sight and smell of the dead mare would be enough to deter any other horses.

Luke heard the foal nickering again, and turned to see it trotting into the distance. He felt a wave of sadness as he watched it disappear, alone, into the harsh ragged country. 'I thought you were just a dream, Rusty.'

Bob recoiled in disgust when he saw Luke and realised what was making the flies stick to him.

'I need water,' was all Luke could whisper, pushing past him and heading for the river.

'What's all that blood on you?' Tyson demanded, grabbing Luke by the arm and swinging him around to face him.

'It's from a horse,' Luke explained as the three men crowded around.

Tyson seemed to relax a little, but Tex's face went as still as stone and he began to back away, speaking in his own tongue, with words like *dirty yarramin* and *purri purri*.

'I found a horse stuck in a wire trap,' Luke said. 'I had to cut its throat.'

'Let the boy go,' said Bob to Tyson. 'He needs a drink.'

Tyson relaxed his grip and Luke staggered to the river. He threw himself into the water fully clothed and drank big gulps of water. He scrubbed at his arms and his hands, washing the blood off.

'Are there any crocs around here?' he asked Bob, who squatted on the riverbank watching him with a concerned look on his face. There had been big floods up this way last season and he'd heard stories about saltwater crocodiles being washed upriver onto the stations.

Bob shrugged. 'Freshies, maybe.'

Luke looked at the blood, staining the water around him.

I eat asparagus – nothing can kill me . . .

Tyson came along with his fishing line. 'Hey, Luke, get back over near those tree roots and burley up a barra for me,' he laughed.

Luke peeled his clothes off and chucked them on the bank. 'Swap ya,' he called back, and dived under the water. He ran his hands over his head and rubbed his legs, getting every last trace of the blood off.

When he pulled himself out of the river, Bob threw him an old pair of shorts. Tyson already had his jeans tied to the roots of a big old paperbark tree, floating over the top of the water. 'Gunna get me a biggun,' sang Tyson, casting out.

'That's if you don't scare them all away first,' hissed Bob.

Luke grabbed his boots and began scrubbing at them. He thought of the small red foal, bleating for its mother.

I used to do that. Never brings 'em back.

He went over to the fire to get some food. Tex immediately walked away.

Purri purri.

'He reckons I'm cursed,' said Luke.

Bob raised his eyebrows. 'If you'da seen yourself a minute ago, you'd probably reckon the same thing!'

'It had its whole front end wrapped in barbed wire. What was I s'posed to do?'

'There's a gun in the back of the ute,' said Bob.

'Oh.'

Tex walked back out from the shrubs and passed Luke a box of dry crackers. 'You ever sleep at night, boy?'

'Not much,' said Luke.

Tex spent a moment fiddling about in his tackle box. He rigged up a new handline and then cast it out. 'You should go for a walk with Tyson today. Do you good,' he said finally. 'You need to learn some stuff. Learn with your hands and your body and your mind. Not just with talk.'

It sounded more interesting than fishing.

'Okay,' said Luke. 'Where to?'

'Tyson's a big owl, a teacher; he'll show you some things, show you what you can do in safety, without trespassing on stuff that you don't have any right to see or hear or talk about.'

Luke looked at Tyson, who was gently playing his line out.

Tyson looked up at him. 'What? Now?'

'Uh huh,' said Luke, nodding. He heard Tex chuckle.

A look came over Tyson's face as if he was adjusting his thoughts and reprogramming his day. He shrugged. 'Right.' He dropped his handline and leapt up off the ground in one swift movement. 'Let's go then, furry boy!'

12

LUKE RAN TO catch up with Tyson, who was setting a fast pace. 'Why did you call me a furry boy?'

'That'll come,' said Tyson in a voice that told him to be patient. He walked with his hands in his pockets. 'Now, tell me more about these horses, Luke. What's going on with you and these horses?'

Luke talked. The words came tumbling out as he told Tyson about the photos of his parents, about the horse-gentling program and what Harry had taught him, about Legs, his favourite colt, and about the calmness horses gave him. He talked of Jess and her filly, the min min lights and how they disappeared into the belly of the mare.

Tyson stopped walking and looked him dead in the eye. 'Okay, Luke, so you're not just pony club here.'

'I've never been to pony club,' said Luke.

'Not just stockman, either,' Tyson continued. 'The

way you have with these horses. You've got dream there, you and this Jess girl. You're stepping into things you got no idea about.'

'Dream? Why, because of the min min lights?' Luke put his hands in the air, totally confused. 'Why don't you like horses?'

Tyson screwed up his face. 'It just sounds like *purri purri* to me.'

'You think I'm cursed too?' Luke would have laughed if Tyson hadn't looked so deadly serious. He screwed up his nose. 'They're just horses!'

Tyson shook his head. 'You haven't got a clue, have you? You got that big horse dream kicking around inside you, and you got no idea what to do with it. You don't know who you are or where you're from.'

'You're right, I don't,' Luke said flatly.

'That dream you got inside you, that could be your old ones, trying to claim you.'

'Old ones?'

'Yeah, like your ancestors.'

'I'm not Aboriginal,' said Luke. 'I don't have ancestors in the land who look after me.'

'You don't need to be Aboriginal. If you can find that connection with the land, you can link back to your own ancestors, find your own way. Way back in iron-age Britain, there were tribes of horsemen. They were warriors, Luke. They had red hair, just like you, and they fought the Romans. Their totem was horse and wolf.'

'My hair's not red.'

Tyson rolled his eyes. 'What, is it strawberry-blonde, then? You a pretty boy or something?'

'It's just brown . . . kinda reddish-brown.'

'Chestnut, like a horse, whatever,' said Tyson. 'Come, walk with me, I'll show you some things.'

Luke folded his arms across his chest and stood his ground.

'What?' asked Tyson.

'We're not going to find British ancestors in Australia.'

'Maybe we won't. Maybe we will. Maybe we'll find a connection that runs right through to the navel of the world at Uluru, and from there to England.'

Luke unfolded his arms and followed Tyson reluctantly. Iron-age warriors. This ought to be good.

'Now, this thing I'm showing you, it's not sorcery – none of that dirty stuff. This is just how people connect.' Tyson gestured for Luke to come up beside him. 'Look how you're walking! Do you even know where you're putting your feet?'

Luke looked down at his feet, as he picked his way over the rough ground. They were lily-white and stinging from all the sticks and brambles and stones.

Tyson stopped again. 'Put your feet on the ground.'

He put his hands on Luke's shoulders and repositioned him. 'You have four places in your body that hold power,' he explained, 'and your feet are one of them. You gotta get those shoes off and feel that dirt.'

'They *are* off.'

'Then plant your feet, really plant them.'

Luke wriggled his toes. The ground felt hot and dry and uneven.

'Now, clap your hands a few times.'

Luke gave a few half-hearted claps, not sure whether to hold his hands in front of him or up in the air. He felt a bit stupid.

Tyson rolled his eyes again. 'Give it a bit more grunt.'

Luke clapped again, harder this time, in front of his belly.

'Bit harder,' said Tyson, still not satisfied.

Luke anchored his feet to the ground and brought his hands crashing together.

'Now, where do you feel that in your body – what part goes tight?'

Luke put a hand below his navel and looked questioningly at Tyson.

'Yeah, right there, behind and underneath your belly button,' said Tyson. 'That place is where you keep your big power, and you'll need it to get your feet going.'

'Big power? Bring it on.'

'Rub your hands together,' instructed Tyson, rubbing his own together to demonstrate. 'Now rub them across your belly, feel it go warmer, tighter.' He leaned over and pushed his own fingers into Luke's stomach. 'Now, bring your fingertips together. Real slow. Stop just before they touch.'

Luke anchored his feet again the way Tyson had showed him and tried to feel the belly power. He brought his fingertips together.

Nothing happened.

Tyson's voice was low and careful. 'Watch close. Keep watching. See something there?'

Luke rubbed his hands together, breathed, anchored his feet and stared at the tiny gap between his fingertips.

'Like smoke or electricity?' Tyson prompted.

A tiny current trickled through the gap, shot down through Luke's legs and earthed at his feet, startling him.

'Keep your feet planted,' Tyson said. 'Let all that bad stuff go down into that dirt. Feel it go deep and give it all to the land.'

Luke closed his eyes and felt suddenly exhausted. He imagined the poison from old wounds that had never quite healed running down the trunk of his body, into the ground, taking with it his grief and his anger. He stood there, letting it drain away.

'Now you find that the land gives back,' said Tyson

quietly. 'Feel the way it feeds power back into you, big, long, deep power. It makes your belly power stronger, like recharging a battery.' His voice was soothing, like a gentle breeze. 'That's your old people looking after you.'

Luke opened his eyes and tilted his head. 'This is crazy,' he said. 'I don't have any old people. I don't have family.'

'Yes, you do, Luke, or you wouldn't be standing here. You just gotta find 'em,' said Tyson. 'You gotta let 'em find you. They're right here, in the land. You connect deep enough, you'll find 'em.' He walked around Luke. 'Now I'm going to hit you, but don't let go of your belly power, your feet or the land.'

Luke focused on connecting his feet to the earth again.

Tyson sank his fist into Luke's belly. Hard. Harder than Luke expected.

Luke took in the shock of it and sent it shooting through his feet and into the ground. He heard a roaring sound in his ears as he did so, and he wondered if it was the breath being knocked from his lungs or the angry cries of iron-age warriors, somewhere in his subconscious.

Still steady on his feet, he looked up at Tyson, unsure of what had just happened.

'There! That should have knocked you down.' Tyson sounded pleased with him. 'Now, think you can walk and still stay connected to the land this way? Try it.'

Luke walked off, staring at his feet as though trying a new pair of shoes.

'Light but solid,' said Tyson. 'Yeah, you're really walking on the land now.' He gave Luke a rough shove on the shoulder. 'See! You got your male power back to its house, in your belly, and reconnected it with its family there in the earth!'

Luke walked through a few more shoves and punches. Before long he began to feel exhausted. It took a lot of concentration.

'You're all over this,' laughed Tyson, belting him again. And then again, apparently just for the heck of it.

'Yeah, righto,' said Luke, raising an arm to protect himself.

Tyson laughed, a deep booming laugh that echoed into the distant skies and filled the world with joy. He walked alongside Luke, his crazy hair springing in all directions.

Luke couldn't stop a small laugh escaping. 'Nut-job,' he mumbled.

As he walked, he imagined tribes of horsemen, warriors, with red hair, lending him their strength and for the first time in weeks, he felt connected to something, something that no one could ever take away.

Tyson grinned at him. 'All right?'

Luke nodded. 'Yeah.'

He was full of something, something he couldn't explain. His past, his present and his future were fusing together. And it felt okay. It felt good.

'We're all one thing, boy, and when we break off – no good!'

That night, Luke feasted on black bream that Tex and Bob had pulled from the river. They showed him how to scale and gut the fish, and how to get the coals to glow just right before digging a shallow hole and using it as an oven, with the coals shovelled back on top. They roasted the fish whole and ate them with the leftover yams, seasoned with a day's worth of hunger.

Later, Luke sat with his blanket wrapped around him, staring into the fire. He fingered the moonstone around his neck and thought of Jess. He wished she was there to talk to.

She would love it out here.

He thought of ancestors and spirits and horses and strangely, of metal: of steel and roaring furnaces; the heavy clanking of a blacksmith's hammer over an anvil. And then he slept.

13

HE WAS WOKEN BY snuffling on his head. It worked its way over his forehead, around his ear and blew inquisitive puffs over his cheek.

Legsy?

It was a nice way to be woken up. He smiled before he opened his eyes as he felt the colt's lip on his cheek.

'What are you doing out of your stable?'

He opened his eyes, and a dark red horse startled so fast that it nearly left its legs behind. It galloped off into the distance, sending clouds of dust behind it. It was one of the funniest things Luke had ever seen and he laughed out loud as he sat up.

'A brumby sniffed me!'

Looking around, Luke rubbed his hand over his head. He was at the base of some hills again. Had he sleep-walked?

From the hillside, the red horse snorted at him, tossed

its head, then scrambled up and over the peak.

Luke jumped up and began to jog after it. When he got to the top of the hill, he smelled the dead mare. In the valley near the trap, a dozen or so horses circled the carcass, their heads low, watching. Further out, mares with their foals at foot stood quietly, swishing their tails and occasionally shaking their heads to get rid of the flies.

The dark red horse walked back and forth between the mares, sniffing at the air as if to say, *I know you're up there.*

Suddenly, it galloped straight at Luke and stamped both front feet on the ground, snorting.

'They're all yours, big fella,' he said, taking a step back. 'I'm not gonna touch 'em.'

The stallion walked back to the mob and singled out a small red foal, nuzzling it and pushing it towards the middle of the mob. Luke could see now that it was a colt. Two other mares went to it and ushered it close.

'Rusty,' he whispered. Then he smiled. 'You got taken in by the mob. Good for you, little man.'

He could see the similarities between the colt and the stallion. Both were deep red, although he couldn't be sure that wasn't just the dust covering them. They both had large cheekbones and a narrow face; long sloping shoulders, short backs and rounded hindquarters. The colt had a tiny white dot on his forehead, the stallion a wide white blaze that ran the length of his face and down between his nostrils. He was harsh, wild and shrewd, like the land around him, and he circled his mares possessively. His feet reached out and covered the hard unforgiving rocks in long, rangy strides.

Suddenly he wheeled and rushed at Luke again, coming closer this time. Luke took his warning. He retreated slowly down the other side of the hill, checking behind him as he went, until he was some distance away; then he ran, sending little avalanches of rocks tumbling about his ankles as he went.

He went back to the river and sat against a tree, watching the top of the hill, knowing that the stallion would come checking again soon. The image of the horses crowded his mind. It was almost as if they were paying their respects.

'It was like a funeral or something,' he said to Bob. 'They were grieving.'

'Yeah, they're different in the wild,' Bob said. 'Around the homesteads, we bury dead horses quick as we can. They never get a chance to grieve like that.'

Luke thought of the stallion: his gentleness as he nuzzled the colt and led it to the centre of the mares. He thought of Biyanga, pacing about in his stable at home.

He would kill a foal if he got near one. He wouldn't even know if it was his.

That afternoon, while the other men fished, Luke walked back to the top of the hill. The mob was still there, surrounding the dead mare. They left only to drink at the creek, a few at a time, and then resumed their vigil over the body. It was the most incredible thing he had ever witnessed. If only he could ring Jess and tell her about it. She could spend a whole century sitting under trees and watching horses around here.

Before long, Tyson joined him. The man puffed as he climbed up the rocky hillside. 'What are you doin' all the way up here?' he said, reaching the top and grabbing hold of a small tree to steady himself while he got his breath back. 'Tryin' to kill me?'

'Watching the brumbies,' smiled Luke.

'Coming for another walk? Got more to show you.' Tyson pulled a comical face. 'Soon as those ancestors send some air my way.'

'You wanna cut down on the muesli bars, mate.'

'I'm waiting for you to catch a barra so I can,' said Tyson. He let go of the tree and set off across the top of the ridge. 'Coming?'

Luke took a last glance at the brumbies and followed him.

Tyson went over the belly power again and then showed Luke how to bring that heat back into his hands, and how to hold them in front, palms out, sending ripples of energy shooting through his fingers in crooked waves out into the land.

Luke learned how to bring all that power, the heat from his hands, the tingling from his feet, the tightness from his belly, and send it blazing up into his eyes.

At one point a low menacing wolf-like growl escaped involuntarily from his throat, making Tyson step back and look at him with mild alarm. 'Geez, bro, you're scarin' me!'

Luke shook slightly and laughed, a little nervously. 'Whoa. Where did that come from?'

'If you can put those eyes on whenever you want, you'll probably never have to fight again,' said Tyson. 'And if somebody does hit you and your feet are planted, you won't fall.'

Luke remembered the other day, when he had slashed Tyson with the knife. It had been like striking a stone. Tyson hadn't moved. 'Can we walk some more?' he asked.

'Sure,' said Tyson, 'But when you walk, keep your belly power strong. Don't walk like a loser anymore.'

As they continued, Tyson told him how to connect through his head. 'Last thing is the sky,' he said, standing on top of the mountain with the wind swirling through his untameable hair. 'You can connect that way too, from your head, feel that power come up from feet, let it go straight up to the sky, like you're just hanging there on a string.' He raised his chin and held out his arms. You don't even have to be walking to connect with the earth. You can be on a motorbike or a horse.'

Luke held out his arms and joined him.

'That's it,' said Tyson. 'Your head is like your feet for the sky.'

'My mother is in the sky,' said Luke. 'That's what everyone told me when she died.'

She seemed so far away, so long ago. But he liked that he could imagine her arms around him, like the two of them were on the back of that horse again, like in the photo. He could just close his eyes and feel protected. 'I do have ancestors.'

'You got old ones,' Tyson assured him. 'But it's your choice to make. Connect or disconnect. Be something, be nothing. Be somewhere, be nowhere. Up to you. Keep your belly power solid, listen for them, watch for messages, and your old people will come for you, put you on the right track.'

14

THE NEXT DAY, Luke jogged across the wide open country to the hills again. Once on the other side, he followed the brumbies into flatter country, where the soil was brownish-grey and grass grew under a low open forest.

The brumbies knew he was there.

One small brown mare, heavy with foal, seemed to be the leader. She stayed in the centre of the mob and another seven or so circled her, protecting her at all times. Luke wondered why they all followed her. There was nothing powerful or impressive about her. She didn't blow her nostrils or stamp her feet; she didn't bite or kick or charge at the others. She just calmly ate and when she moved on, the others moved on with her.

When Luke made too much noise, she was the first to startle and lead the others to a safer place. Late in the afternoon, she took them to water to drink, and she led them to higher ground when the sun began to sink behind the hills and it grew cold. Even the big red stallion seemed to follow her.

The stallion, he noticed, always stayed at the rear of the group, protecting them, pushing forward any stragglers or frail ones. He was so different from Biyanga at home. The young foals all seemed eager to be around him, stretching out their necks and snapping their gums. He was gentle and playful with them.

Rusty seemed to go from mare to mare, each of whom took turns looking after him. When he slept, stretched out with his eyes closed, absorbing the sun, the mares would keep their ears tuned in his direction.

He had friends his own age, too. The other foals would canter up and invite him to play, then gallop about on the outskirts of the herd, bucking and frolicking. They would rear up and paddle their legs, or nip at each others' flanks as they trotted past.

Luke couldn't get enough of their antics. He jogged over to the hills every day and followed them vast distances along the creeks and into the forests.

It was on the third day of watching them, around midday, that he felt a hand on his shoulder. Bob crouched down next to him.

'Check out the brown mare,' said Luke, pointing to her. 'She's the boss. Wouldn't pick it, would you?'

'Yeah, it's all about the knowledge. They know who the clever one is,' said Bob. 'Same way my mob. Youngsters know who to follow and watch and learn from.'

'They follow her everywhere,' Luke marvelled. 'I can't work out why.'

'They use a lot of body language. See that colt over there?' asked Bob, pointing to a young chocolate horse grazing on the outskirts of the mob. 'He's in big trouble with 'em. Don't know what he did wrong, but that mare's not happy with him. See how she keeps her back to him?'

Luke looked at her; sure enough, her back was to the colt. She shifted every time he tried to approach. 'He plays too rough. The little ones are scared of him.'

'He'll have to go away and learn what he did wrong before she's gonna let him back in,' said Bob.

'I can't work out which foal belongs to what mare,' said Luke. 'They all seem to look after each other.'

Bob nodded. 'The aunties look after the young ones so their mum can have a break – she'll go and graze some better pasture on her own, or have a lay-down. Everyone in the mob helps to raise the young one, keep it safe, teach it how to sense danger. Growing up is not just about getting the mother's milk. The young ones gotta learn how to be part of the group.'

Luke got the distinct feeling Bob was trying to tell him something. 'Same way your mob?'

Bob nodded. 'The longer you stay with your mob, the better protected you are. Young ones can't predict danger like the old ones can.' He looked pointedly at Luke. 'You stay with your brothers until you're ready. They'll guide you and protect you.'

'Yeah, well, that'd be good if I *had* any brothers,' said Luke.

'You got brothers back home, Luke.' Bob frowned at him. 'You should send Lawson a message, let him know you're all right. Your family got enough sorry business right now, losing the old one like that. Sometimes it's good to go off and learn with your cousins and your uncles, but then you go back, Luke. They're your family.'

A dozen faces flashed through Luke's mind. Harry, Annie, Lawson, Ryan, all his friends. 'I'm not blood with them, Bob. I don't know if they even want me there.'

'Luke,' Bob said gently, 'blood family's not the only kind of family you can have. Our way, we got all sorts of kinship: skin names, totems. They map out where you fit in life and how you relate to everyone else.'

'We're all connected through the horses,' said Luke. He smiled suddenly. 'Same way my mob!'

Bob grinned and nodded. 'Same way your mob!'

Bob pointed to a small bay filly. 'You see that young filly there? The day she comes in season, that old red stallion will kick her out. Out over the hills there, there'll be a mob of bachelor colts ready to take her in. One of them will take her for himself.'

He waggled a finger at Luke and grinned. 'But not until she's come of age, or until her father says so – you got that bit too?'

Luke screwed up his nose.

'Why d'you look like that?' laughed Bob. 'You got a girl back home?'

Luke looked away. 'Nah.'

Bob raised his eyebrows.

'She's just a good friend, that's all.'

Bob stood up and slapped Luke on the shoulder. 'Let's go back to camp. Show you how to catch a fish!'

That evening, Luke held the reel in his left hand the way Bob had shown him. With his other hand, he twirled the hook and sinkers around his head and flung it out to the river. It snapped back at him, narrowly missing Tex's face and snagging in the tree behind him.

'Hey!' said Tex in alarm, reeling backwards. 'You're holding it wrong. Turn it out the other way so the line can come off.'

'Sorry.' Luke pulled at the line, trying to yank the hook out of the tree. He was determined to catch a fish.

He *had* to. Tyson had eaten every other morsel of food in the camp. The options were either to catch a fish or eat dry noodles.

'Snagged *again*,' Tex grumbled, tugging at the line from every direction. It snapped and a thread of fishing line hung from the end of Luke's reel like a broken spider web. 'I reckon there's an old stump down there that looks like a Christmas tree with all my lures on it.'

Luke laid his reel on the bank of the river, then pulled off his shirt. 'I'm going in.'

Tyson walked past with an assortment of reels and tackle in one hand. 'You got those feet connected, boy?' he enquired, before swinging his fist into Luke's belly.

Luke managed to brace himself, but had nowhere near the connection he'd had the other day. He got his breath back and stood straight again.

'Yep,' he wheezed.

Tyson walked on along the riverbank. 'Big old barra, here I come,' he said in a sing-song voice.

'I'm headed north tomorrow, Luke,' said Bob, squatting next to him. 'Where you headed? You want me to drop you back in Isa?'

'What are Tyson and Tex doing?' Luke asked, hoping they would be staying on the river a while longer. He wanted to keep watching the brumbies, especially Rusty.

'They've both got families and jobs they gotta get

back to,' said Bob. 'I'll be mustering up there all week for a local campdraft. I could ask the boss if he's got any more work.'

Luke thought about it. He had hardly any money and he was getting sick of sleeping on the ground. Clean clothes would be good, too. He'd been living in the old shorts Bob had given him and not much else. His jeans were beyond redemption. But he wanted to watch the brumbies some more.

'When's the draft?'

'Next weekend,' said Bob.

'Can I meet you there?' One more week without money or clothes wouldn't hurt . . .

Bob shrugged. 'Yeah. Tyson's driving to the shop. I'll get him to pick up some tucker for you, hey.' He looked at the reel in Luke's hand. 'You might get a bit hungry otherwise.'

'Hey, reckon you could get me a ride at that draft?' asked Luke. It was one way to get money – win it.

Bob pulled a *maybe* face. 'See what I can do.'

15

THE NEXT MORNING, Luke rushed to the edge of the clearing where Tyson was stepping into the big twin cab. 'Tyson, wait up!'

Tyson held out his hand and shook Luke's urban style again. 'You keep your belly power strong, ay,' he said, 'and when you go near them horses, it'll tell you if it's a good one or a bad one. If you feel it pulling, follow it. You still connected?'

Luke grinned and nodded, knowing what was coming next.

Tyson swung a fist into his belly and, as Luke twisted to deflect it, it connected heavily with his ribs. He staggered backwards. 'Oh, geez.' He sank to the ground, clutching his ribs.

Tyson looked puzzled. 'Where were your feet, boy?'

'Ohhh,' Luke moaned. 'I think you broke something.'

Tex pulled himself across the bench seat of the twin

cab and peered out the open window. 'Bloody 'ell, Tyson,' he grumbled. 'Whatcha done to the little fulla *now*?'

Luke writhed on the ground. Tyson squatted next to him. 'I didn't think I got you *that* bad.'

Tex got out of the ute. 'Let me have a look,' he said, prising Luke's hands from his chest and lifting his shirt.

Luke opened one eye. 'Is it bad?' he croaked.

A wave of seriousness washed over the men as they looked over his ribs. Tex looked perplexed. 'Can't tell,' he said. 'How many lumps you have before?'

Luke let out a painful wheeze. 'Just three,' he lied.

Tex, with a look of intense concentration, poked at the various lumps and counted. 'You got more than that 'ere, now.' His face turned thunderous and he swore as he slapped Tyson hard across the back of the head. 'Go ring the flying doctors, *now*,' he ordered. 'You probably punctured his lung!'

Luke rolled away from Tyson. He couldn't keep a straight face for much longer.

'Can you breathe okay?' asked Tyson.

'Just find a phone,' snapped Tex.

Luke nearly choked as a laugh escaped him. He tried to mask it as cries of agony. He caught a glimpse of Tyson's frowning face and couldn't help chuckling loudly. His ribs had never been so funny before. 'Gotcha,' he squeaked.

'You cheeky little . . .'

Behind Tyson, Tex hissed and chugged so hard he sounded as though he would split at the seams. Bob leaned against his ute, one hand over his mouth, trying to hide a smirk. But his welling eyes gave him away.

Tyson walked back to the twin-cab. He yanked the back door open, pulled out his swag and threw it on top of Luke, following it with a bag of instant oats. 'Here, have some more horse food,' he said, lobbing them at Luke's head.

Luke ducked under the swag and deflected the oats. When he looked out the other side, Tyson was stepping into the driver's seat.

The wild-haired man grinned and started the engine. 'The best teachers learn from their students, ay. You got me a good one.' He ran a hand gingerly over his left shoulder. 'You got me a *couple* of good ones. I won't forget.'

'Thanks, Tyson,' Luke said. 'You got me some good ones too.'

'Listen to your belly.' Tyson winked as he put the ute in gear. 'It'll keep you safe.'

Tex leaned across Tyson. 'Don't go too far from the river.'

The car rolled away over the bumpy earth and across the causeway.

Bob kicked dirt over the last coals of the fire and threw his swag in the back of his ute. 'So, I'll see you at the draft. Plenty of trucks'll be headed up there. You just hitch a ride, ay?'

'Yeah, yeah,' said Luke, nodding.

'If you get in any trouble, there's an Aboriginal settlement about a half day's walk up the river,' said Bob. 'It's on the way to the draft. Just follow the green suitcases. And tell 'em I sent you.'

'Okay,' said Luke, wondering what on earth green suitcases could be.

Bob looked him over again. 'I might stop out if I get time, ay? See if you caught a barra yet.'

'Better bring some hot chips,' said Luke.

The following day was still new and untouched, with only a few birds beginning to twitter, when Luke threw on his backpack and set off towards the hills again. His first night alone at the remote river crossing had been long and sleepless, a mix of anxiety tempered by the excitement of seeing the brumbies again. All night he had thought about them and the way they looked after each other and fought and bickered, just like a real family. He could think of nothing but seeing Rusty again. It was as though he had lost the controls; someone or some*thing* else was driving him.

He found the mob in a small valley. The mares were lying down with their foals while the stallion and the older colts grazed quietly around them. The chocolate one, he noticed, still grazed on the outer.

Luke scanned the clearing, looking for the little red colt. Several of the mares turned their ears towards him. One stood up. The others kept grazing as though they knew he was there, but perceived no threat.

He soaked in the sounds of the valley: the soft contented snort of a sleepy horse, the swish of a tail. He studied the horses intently, watching the tiny signals they sent each other. The slight turning of one mare's head away from another established her place in the ranking system; a turn of a colt's ear showed that he was checking the boundaries for signs of danger; the lift of one mare's chin told another mare's foal to stay away.

But where was Rusty? In the half-light of the breaking day, the foals were just small dark blobs, curled up next to their mothers.

A small shadow slunk between two trees.

Luke strained his eyes to see, but whatever it was had disappeared. From the corner of his eye, he saw another shadow slide between clumps of grass. He spun his head around. There were three more shadows lurking. Dingos. They were everywhere.

He jumped to his feet. There were at least six dogs

prowling around in a pack. The stallion stepped to the edge of the mob and held his nose up to the wind. The little brown mare scrambled to her feet, whinnying. Like dominoes in reverse, the others followed. They stood alert with their ears pricked, sniffing at the air.

The brown mare trotted a few steps beyond the mob. She spun around to put her rump to the dingos and lashed out with a hind leg, warning them to stay away.

The dogs kept circling, snarling, panting, dodging back and forth. The foals skittered about nervously, brushing up close to their mothers. Rusty erupted suddenly from a patch of tall grass, ran into the centre of the mob and gave a frightened whinny.

Luke picked up a handful of stones and threw them at one of the dark shapes. 'Get out of here!' he hissed. He didn't want to make a big commotion and frighten the horses into a gallop. The dogs would only give chase.

As the dogs advanced into the clearing on slinky hind-quarters, their lips curled into snarls, the horses crushed together, panicky. They lashed out with their hind legs as the dogs darted in and snapped at their heels. The old red stallion charged one of them and stamped his feet. It snarled viciously and rushed back at him. The stallion spun and lashed out at it with a back foot, sending the dog flying with a yelp.

The noise startled the mares and they fled across

the gully, only to be met by more dogs. Confused, they scattered in all directions. Luke saw Rusty get separated from the mob. One dog turned its attention on him and two other dogs followed, sprinting and growling, surrounding him.

Luke ran up to them, throwing rocks. 'Get out of it! Leave him alone!' His attempts to help only added to the chaos, scattering the horses further. He watched them gallop into the hills with the dogs on their heels.

Two dogs sprinted after Rusty and another came in from the side, aiming for his head. The young chocolate colt came out of nowhere and snatched one of them in his teeth. He shook it like a rag doll while it howled with pain, and then flung it on a rock with a bone-shattering crunch. Then the colt spun around and hoofed a second dog in the head. It went to the ground like a bag of rocks. The third dog fled, its tail between its legs.

'Way to go, Chocky!' yelled Luke. He hurled another handful of stones at the remaining dogs as they scattered and fled. 'And don't come back!'

The mares came galloping out of the tree-covered hillside, calling for their foals. They skittered anxiously back to their mothers while the colts circled protectively around them, pushing them back up into a group.

Chocky nickered gently to Rusty and guided him back to the mob. The mares welcomed the little colt back into their circle, and nuzzled and sniffed all over Chocky. He stood with his tail in the air and gave an impressive snort.

'Chocky! You're a hero!' said Luke out loud.

The little brown mare stepped up to Chocky, sniffed him briefly on the nose and then walked away, inviting him to follow. She led him into the centre of the mob and together they resumed grazing.

Luke wandered over to the dog to check it was properly dead. He nudged the black lump with one foot. It was a bitch, with a full udder of milk, and it was very dead.

Her pups are going to be hungry.

The nights by the river were long and empty. Luke tried to fill in the silence by making up bad hip-hop tunes and beat boxing.

I'm sitting on a river (much scratching and snaring)
In the middle of the world (more scratching and snaring)
I wish I had some food (quick K-snare, inward hollow snare, nearly choked)
And my favourite Jessy-girl! (back to scratching and snaring)

He sounded appalling against the serene backdrop,

but he was beyond caring. At least it frightened the cane toads away.

Each day, as Luke watched the brumbies, he made some time to kick off his boots and just stand on the land.

Heat from your hands, tingle from your feet, tightness from your belly . . .

He would think of Harry and feed all his sorrow back down into the dirt. Then he would try to pull all that the man had given him – strength, energy, self-belief – up out of the ground.

Each night he thought less and less of the company of the other men, and more and more of his family. His mob. As he rolled into his swag, he took the moonstone out, then fell asleep with it in his hand, listening to the sounds of the river. And when he dreamt, they were beautiful dreams. He was lying in his own river, the Coachwood River. Harry, Annie, Lawson and Ryan, Tom and Jess, Rosie and even Grace were never far away.

16

TWO DAYS BEFORE he was due to meet Bob, Luke woke after sleeping so soundly he barely knew where the night had gone. Darkness was shifting into day and the air was still and cool. He rose from his swag and dived into the river, letting it wash over him and clear his groggy head. He lay face-up with his arms pulling slowly back and forth through the water, watching the day slowly take on more colour.

Above the tree branches, silvery locusts flitted in the early sunlight. Birds came down to the water to quench their thirst, then rose again, darting in and out of the leaves. On the edge of the river, a small fresh-water crocodile hid from the sun under the overhanging branches.

As Luke lay there watching it, thinking about ancestors and the land, he held his belly firm and felt the earth breathing all around him.

Then a low thrumming noise crept slowly into his consciousness. He instantly felt a twist in his belly and knew something wasn't right.

Listen to your belly. It will keep you safe.

He pulled himself out of the water and walked hurriedly over to his boots, pulled them on and headed out into the open field beyond the river.

A small white helicopter skimmed along the paddock. Luke could see two people in the seats, as clear as day. It slowed, hovered momentarily, and then continued whizzing across the ground. It went up and over the hills and disappeared behind them into the rugged limestone country and off the pasture lease.

There were no cattle over those hills. That chopper was going after the brumbies!

Luke broke into a jog and quickly progressed to a sprint. He ran and ran until his breath tore at his lungs, drowning out the sound of the helicopter, which chugged away behind the hills. He grabbed a post at the edge of the paddock, leapt over the fence and began to scrambling up the hill, stumbling and tripping in his haste.

At the summit he saw the chopper again, low over the tree-lined creek. It hovered up and down and zigzagged from side to side.

The brumbies cantered along the edge of the creek, staying under the cover of the trees.

Luke ran along the top of the ridge, trying to keep up.

'That's it, stay on the river, Rusty,' he said out loud as he dodged, bare-legged, in and out of spinifex bushes.

The brumbies reached a bend in the creek, and the little brown mare shot out from the trees and galloped across the flat plains. Two other horses followed and soon the whole mob was racing across the hard, dry savannah, out in the open, vulnerable.

'No!' Luke yelled helplessly. 'Don't come out or they'll shoot you!'

He ran down the side of the hill, waving at the chopper, hoping to place himself between it and the mob, but they were drawing further and further away.

He scrambled down the hillside, and began to lose control of his feet as rocks rolled out from under him. He tumbled, faster and faster, until he could barely get one foot in front of another. Low spiky bushes scratched at his legs.

Then a large rock dislodged under his foot and sent him crashing forward, trying to brace his fall with his right hand but rolling over and onwards. The thousand torturous needles of spinifex bush brought him to a sudden and mute-rendering halt. His wrist hammered with big, excruciating belts of pain, and his spike-peppered skin screeched in protest with any movement he made.

He gasped for breath, and when he finally filled his lungs he swore as loud and hard as he could. Then he gritted his teeth and with his good left arm, he managed to pull himself out of the spinifex bush, tearing his shirt to shreds and gathering more spikes in the process. He stood clutching his right arm and cursing, over and over.

You still connected, boy?

'No, I'm bloody not,' he yelled angrily at the land. In the distance, the horses were still galloping, leaving streams of dust behind them. The helicopter was directly above them. But it wasn't shooting.

What did those people want? They'd run the brumbies into the ground. Luke held his wrist and began walking after them with Tyson's voice echoing in his ears.

Don't walk like a loser anymore.

He stopped, glanced down at his boots and considered taking them off. Then he looked at the rough country ahead of him. He decided to keep his boots on, but he pushed them as deep into the soil as he could. The immense tableland, covered in grasses, growing out of ancient, cracked brown soil, was lined with fissures that carried the sky and the rivers and the past and the future deep down into the earth, all as one, the rocks and the trees and the canyons and gorges. Luke connected his feet to that earth and felt his body become a part of it.

He brought his fingertips together and sent the long nauseating waves of pain through his wrist down into his feet and emptied it into the land.

And then he felt it: the long, deep energy of the land, his ancestors, looking after him. Feeling strengthened, he walked, keeping to the western side of the hill where the morning sun had not yet hit.

Below him, the chopper seemed to be using the gully and a fenceline to channel the brumbies. Their pace was slowing, and Luke could see the stallion nipping at the old stragglers. A ball of red rolled in a cloud of dust. The stallion barely had time to leap over the top of it.

'Rusty!'

Luke could see the little colt lying in a twisted heap. He quickened his pace to a painful jog and ran for what seemed like hours.

'Easy, fella,' panted Luke, as he reached him.

The colt lifted his head and rolled his eyes in panic.

'Easy, boy, you're going to have to trust me.'

The colt thrashed about and tried to get up. Luke crouched down and clutched his wrist, which was making him feel queasy again. He looked away from the colt and tried to let him calm, but Rusty snorted wildly with every breath.

Luke crouched lower and turned his back completely, trying to look unthreatening. He inched backwards towards the colt, but the closer he got the more panicked Rusty became.

'You and I are gonna be good friends, little man,' said Luke quietly. 'No one's gonna hurt you.'

The colt bawled a long, terrified cry to its mob.

'You don't want to go where they're going, Rusty, you really don't.'

The colt screamed again.

Luke took a moment to think. Rusty wasn't a big animal – he could easily pin the colt to the ground and forcibly handle him until he was completely desensitised and submissive, then use the scraps of his shirt as a rope to lead him away. Or he could help Rusty up and allow him the same destiny that awaited the rest of his mob: slaughteryards or rodeos.

Luke clutched his arm to his chest. All that channelling into the ground wasn't easy when he was in so much pain he could hardly see straight, and trying to gentle a panic-stricken brumby at the same time. He held the back of his good hand out towards the colt. 'Easy, fella.'

Rusty panicked. He scrambled to his feet and limped away with his nose in the air, calling desperately after the mob.

The helicopter rose up from the horizon and Luke watched helplessly as it came back for the colt, rounding him up with the rest of the mob.

17

THE SUN WAS SETTING by the time Luke found the settlement Bob had spoken of. He stumbled up over the riverbank and saw a row of houses, set side by side behind chain mesh fences.

He headed up the red dirt road, past a collection of old car bodies and some empty green wine casks scattered about among other rubbish.

A big grey horse wandered into the carport of one of the homes and licked at a tap. Two men sat side by side in chairs on a lawn, under the shade of a big tree, looking out onto the street. They stopped talking when Luke walked past. He nodded at them, and they hesitated before nodding back.

Further up the street, two small boys in football jerseys kicked a ball around.

Luke clutched his right arm with his other hand. His

wrist was swollen and painful; he was pretty sure it was broken. He walked back towards the two men.

'My friend Bob told me to come here if I got in any trouble,' he said.

One of the men stood up and came over. He cast a wary eye over Luke as his mate joined him.

'Bob who?'

It was only then that Luke realised how he must look. His shirt was torn to shreds, and so was most of his body. He was filthy.

'Umm. Bob. The stockman.'

'Oh yeah, yeah.' Both men nodded enthusiastically. 'Bob Stockman.' One offered his hand and such was his relief, Luke smiled and automatically held out his own. The man shook it enthusiastically.

He didn't catch the man's name. The pain swam over him, caught the words and distorted them, making them seem close but far away at the same time.

The next thing Luke knew, he was on his back looking up at a dozen or so black faces, all talking at once. The man who had shaken his hand stared down at him. 'You plenty busted up, little fulla,' he said in a deep voice.

Luke just nodded.

The hand-shaker turned to one of the kids. 'Better get the grey nurse.'

'Yeah, Sister Suzie fix you up,' a boy said.

'Yeah, Sister Suzie, Sister Suzie,' the kids all began chanting. 'Go and get Sister Suzie!'

Two boys sprinted off up the road.

Luke tried to sit up but a wave of nausea sent him straight back down again. 'Whoa,' he muttered, closing his eyes and clutching his arm.

Minutes later, a four-wheel drive pulled up and a middle-aged white woman jumped out and slammed the door. Her clothes were not a nurse's uniform and her hair was not grey. She took one look at Luke and began issuing orders. 'Which one of you boys is going to run to the store and get some ice?' Without waiting for an answer, she knelt beside Luke and took his arm. 'Get my bag out of the truck for me,' she said to another kid. 'What happened?' she asked the men.

They both looked at her blankly and shrugged their shoulders. 'He just appeared out of nowhere,' the hand-shaker said. 'He was busted up like this when we found him. Says he knows Bob Stockman.'

'Oh,' said the woman. She looked at Luke. 'Are you an artist too?'

'An artist?'

A gaggle of children came running back down the road with a plastic tray of ice. They proudly handed it to Sister Suzie.

'No, no, that won't do. I meant a big bag.' She held her

hands out to match the size and shape of a pillow. 'Big! Go, go quickly. This man is in pain.' She turned to him. 'Your name?'

'Luke Matheson. I'm not an art—'

'I'll just give you an IM for the pain.' She reached into her bag and began loading a needle and syringe. 'So, what brings you to the Gulf?'

'Umm . . .'

'No need to talk,' she said. 'You're exhausted. Do you have any allergies?'

Luke glanced dazedly around him. He knew at some stage he had fainted, but he wasn't quite sure if he had woken up yet. He jumped as Sister Suzie jabbed him in the upper arm with the needle. Yep! Wide awake!

'Sonny, run up to the hospital. Tell them I'm bringing in a fractured arm. Tell the RNs we need an X-ray. Better tell ED we might need RFDS. Tell them OT will need to be notified and P and P might need to be done.'

Sister Suzie watched the kids run up the dirt road towards the hospital. Then she cast a disapproving eye over Luke. 'How old are you?'

'Fifteen, nearly six—'

'And what on earth have you been up to?'

'Umm . . .'

'No, actually, don't tell me,' she said, holding her hands up and cutting him off. 'I don't want to know. You can fill out a form at the hospital. Where are those kids with that ice?' She huffed with impatience. 'Never mind. Get in the car, we'll find some at the hospital. Lucky for you we have a new TMU.'

She lectured him all the way. 'Teenagers lurking about with no purpose in life, getting into trouble . . .'

Luke sat miserably in the front seat, groaning and clutching his arm every time she barrelled through a large pothole without slowing. He was thankful that the hospital was only three streets away.

Hours later, Luke sat in a tall vinyl chair in the waiting room. His arm was set in plaster and resting snugly in a sling. The fracture wasn't complicated, so he didn't have to bother with any of the alphabet Sister Suzie had threatened him with.

TMU stood for tele-medicine unit, he had discovered. It was all done over the internet with a webcam and a big screen. The doctors in Brisbane had looked at his arm and his X-rays and then told the staff that it just needed plaster.

A man with skinny legs and big boots sat opposite Luke. His skin was dark but he also looked slightly Asian. He had dirt and horse hair on his jeans and he held a filthy black hat on his lap. His leg jiggled nervously and his eyes darted about the room.

'Don't know if there's a campdraft on around here, do you?' Luke asked him.

'Yeah, yeah,' the man said, his face lighting up. 'A few kays outta town. At the showgrounds.'

'You riding in it?'

'Yeah. That's if me eyes are still working.' He pointed to his face. 'Gettin' cataracts cut out. You goin'?'

Luke nodded. 'Yeah, might have a ride on a mate's horse. They put many cattle through up here?'

'Few hundred,' the man said.

'They bring 'em in off the stations, do they?'

'Yeah, muster up the scrubbers and the cleanskins, rough cattle, ay,' the man grinned.

'They heli-muster?'

'Yeah.'

'Horses too?'

'A few for the wild horse race – there's rodeo events too, bronc riding an' that.'

Behind the man, out the window, Luke saw a small black horse wander onto the grounds of the hospital and begin picking at the green grass around the sprinklers. 'Who owns all these horses?' he asked. 'Do they just wander around the town?'

'Nobody owns 'em. We just live alongside 'em,' said

143

the man. 'Till the grey nurse threatens to round 'em all up and shoot 'em – then *everybody* owns 'em.'

'Grey nurse?'

The man snorted. 'It's not for the colour of her uniform, ay.' He stood up, his hat in his hand and looked out the window. 'Look, there she goes!' He shook his head.

Outside, the horse trotted around the hospital gardens. Sister Suzie chased it, flapping her arms.

'They any good for riding?' asked Luke.

'Bit skinny. Kids sometimes muck around with 'em.' Then the man crinkled his eyebrows and looked thoughtful. 'If they got fed right they'd probably be okay. There's probably some real good blood running through some of them horses. Out on the stations the brumby stallions sometimes smash the fences to get in with the mares. Or the fences go down in the wet season when there's big floods. The wild horses and the stockhorses get mixed up. Usually the domestic horses come back. But some of 'em are happy to stay out in the bush with the brumbies.'

He looked out the window and started chuckling again. 'That horse has called his brothers in.'

Luke peered out the window. Two more horses had wandered into the yard and Sister Suzie was chasing all three of them with a mop.

18

LUKE FOUND AN external door in what looked like a huge laundry and discreetly discharged himself from the hospital, before anyone could confront him with his medical background, his history with welfare departments and his current state of homelessness.

He located the showgrounds on the outskirts of the settlement, right where the man had told him they'd be. There were stock trucks rolling up already and most of the yards were filled with big grey Brahmans. Several horses were tethered under trees with their saddles on. But he couldn't see any wild horses. He wandered through the yards, the rails of which looked as though they'd been roughly cut from the branches of nearby box gums.

There were some sponsorship banners around the inside of the arena, a large Aboriginal flag, and a shelter at the end built from more local timber and roofed with leafy branches. There were murals with circled dot paintings and dreaming stories painted on a small block building that looked like some sort of canteen. Luke wondered what stories they told.

At the other end of the arena were rodeo chutes, and a big judge's stand with speakers hanging off the sides.

Luke sat under a tree and looked down at his bare legs, his boots with no socks, and what was left of his shirt.

He looked like a complete derelict. How was he going to ride like this? Even up here they must have dress codes.

And then he thought he saw them. A small white truck rumbled past with several horses banging about in a stock crate on the back.

Luke got up and walked after it, trying to catch a glimpse of the horses. They were all ears and noses, peering through the rails of the crate, snorting and whinnying. From the racket, it sounded as though they were loose.

But when a man appeared and let them out, one had a saddle on its back and Luke recognised none of the others.

He walked back to his tree and sat in the heat, swishing flies off himself. More trucks rolled in. He kept an eye out for Bob, but hours later Bob still hadn't appeared.

Some kids began galloping their horses around in a

field opposite, wearing nothing but shorts, toes curled over their stirrup irons. Their bare backs gleamed in the sun.

More cattle trucks rolled into the showgrounds, day slipped into night and still there was no Bob. Several people camped in their trucks and horse floats or settled down under the trees to sleep in swags.

Luke took another of the pills Sister Suzie had given him for the pain and it made him warm, happy and drowsy. He had no blanket or swag, but curled up on his side under the tree and let his eyes close and his mind slow down into stillness.

He woke the next morning to something scratchy rasping over his cheek. A cold, wet bit of rubber snuffled in his ear.

'Oh, yuck, get off me!'

Two pups were licking him. He pulled himself into a sitting position and wiped their slobber off with the back of his good hand.

One pup was yellowy-brown with black points. The other was black all over. Both had coarse fur, bony shoulders and round bellies. They stank.

'They been eating sheep guts,' said a boy standing nearby. He pointed away from the showgrounds to a stand of trees. 'They found a dead sheep over there.'

'Get away from me,' Luke growled at the pups. His wrist throbbed under the plaster and his head hurt.

Both pups jumped on his lap. The yellow one immediately piddled and the black one pulled at his sling, ripping at it with sharp teeth.

'Hey!' yelled Luke. 'You dirty little bugger!' He shoved the incontinent one off his knee and grabbed the toothy one by the scruff of the neck. 'Let go of my sling!'

When it clung on, he pulled his shirt off and scrunched it around its body, together with the sling. Then he flung the whole bundle away.

The black pup rolled around in delight, snarling and yapping at the shirt, its feet waving in the air. Then it pulled at the shirt with its teeth, ripping and growling, until it lay in tatters. Meanwhile, the yellow one slunk a metre away and vomited.

'Take the shirt off my back, why don't you,' said Luke indignantly. He stood up and looked at the patch of piddle that had soaked into his shorts. 'Who owns these dogs?'

A young boy trotted past on a grey horse and burst out laughing. 'Them pups, they pissed all over him!' he called to his friends. 'They're puking everywhere!'

Within minutes, Luke was surrounded by children on

148

their horses. 'Orrr, dis*gust*ing!' they yelled. 'Pworrr!'

Luke swiped at a pup with his boot. 'Where's the closest hose?' he demanded.

'Over there, at the yards. Don't put dog spew in the trough!' the kids sang, galloping off on their horses.

Luke walked after them to the yards, the two pups scampering around his feet. He quickly located the hose and began washing off his pants. 'Trying to take my pants off me too, you little ferals?' he said, squirting the pups in their faces. They yapped and bit at the water gleefully.

'Who owns them?' Luke asked the kids.

'Looks like you do, now,' one of the boys laughed.

'They want to be yours!' said another.

'Not likely,' grumbled Luke. He held the hose over his head and gave his body a quick squirt. 'Get out of it,' he hissed at the pups, lifting his boot sideways at them.

'What you gonna call them, eh, dingo boy?' said the boy on the grey.

'Hydatids and Halitosis,' said Luke flatly. 'Filth and Fang.' As he walked back to the tree, the yellow pup followed closely behind, its big tail wagging happily. Fang darted back and forth snarling at Luke's ankles. Luke stooped, picked up the pup by the scruff of the neck and gave him a good shake. 'If you wanna hang around, you'll have to learn some manners,' he said, looking the pup in the eye. 'Keep those teeth to yourself.'

Fang whimpered, lifted a lip and snarled back.

'What was that?' bellowed Luke.

Fang closed his mouth and wagged his tail sheepishly. Luke tossed him back on the ground. He sat against the tree and both pubs finally settled down and lay quietly at his feet. But Luke couldn't relax. His wrist throbbed and he was starving.

He reached into his pocket and pulled out the small bottle of painkillers. He wrestled it opened and threw one down his throat. Then he pulled out his wallet and teased out his last fifty with his teeth. 'When's someone gonna start cooking some burgers around here?' he asked the pups.

A semitrailer loaded with livestock rolled into the grounds and Luke saw the unmistakeable pointy ears of horses among the bedlam. He got up and followed the truck, then waited anxiously as it lined up the loading ramp and reversed in.

Stockmen hung off the sides of the crate, poking at the cattle with sticks and shooing them out the back door. In the middle of it all, Luke was horrified to see a small brown horse shoot out the gate and down the slippery race. She was panting heavily and nearly bursting with foal.

'Get those horses into another yard,' a stockman yelled. 'That one's gonna foal soon. She needs a drink.'

'Separate those colts and mares,' yelled another.

Luke was relieved to see the stockmen separate the horses from the cattle and put them in separate yards as they unloaded. He ran and jumped up on the rails. Rusty bumped against the brown mare, snapping his gums and bleating in his little goat voice. An old lead was dangling from his neck. There were rope burns around his throat, as though someone had had a go at handling him.

In the next yard, several adult horses bustled around nervously, bunching together at one end of the yard. Chocky pinned his ears back and snorted. The old red stallion was nowhere to be seen.

'Woohooo! It's gonna be a wild, wild horse race this year,' laughed the gate man gleefully, as Chocky lashed at him with a hind leg.

Luke approached the other man. 'What's happening with those ones?' he asked, pointing into Rusty's yard.

'Those ones?' The man pursed his lips and thought about it. 'Not good for much, probably go on an overseas holiday.'

'Holiday?'

'They'll get sold for human consumption. The foreigners love 'em,' said the man.

'People eat horses?'

'They your dogs?' a stockman yelled at Luke.

In another yard, Filth and Fang were lurking about

the heels of some cattle, sending them scurrying about the yard. Fang growled and snapped, while Filth slunk around with his ears back, dodging hooves.

'Nuh, never seen them before,' said Luke, just as Filth bounded over to him with his tongue hanging out the side of his mouth and a stupid grin on his doggy face.

'Get out of here, you mongrel thing,' Luke growled. Fang joined Filth, and the two pups pawed at his bare legs, whimpering.

'Hey, dingo boy! Can my cousin play with your pups?' called the boy on the grey as he rode up to the yard.

'Never seen them before, ay?' the stockman drawled.

Luke shrugged. 'Give you a hundred bucks for that red colt in there,' he offered.

'Yeah, righto.' The man answered so quickly that Luke was sure he would have taken half that.

He looked at the mare, bursting with foal, with sunken flanks and hollows above her eyes. She didn't look good at all. And they were going to truck her to an abattoir.

'How much for the whole pen?'

The man looked at Luke as if he was nuts. 'Gotta feed those pups of yours, ay?' Then he laughed and shrugged. 'Hundred'll cover it, if you want 'em that bad, kid.'

'Can I pay you after the draft?'

'Yeah, s'pose.'

Luke automatically held out his plastered hand to shake but pulled himself up just in time. 'Hang on.' He held out his left hand and offered an awkward cack-handed shake.

The man punched his knuckles. 'They're all yours, mate.'

19

LUKE WALKED BACK to his tree, his mind whirling.

He had to get some prize money. Where on earth was Bob? *God, I hope he's got me a ride. I hope he's got some spare clothes!*

Somewhere a barbecue was heating up and the smell of cooked beef wafted through the air. Luke's stomach growled hungrily. He fingered the fifty in his pocket, knowing he would need it if he didn't get a ride. He wondered how much the prize money was.

He walked to the secretary's tent, behind the rodeo chutes, and took a program. It wasn't big money – a hundred bucks to win the junior, two-fifty for the maiden. And he had no idea what horse Bob might come up with.

The waft of eggs and bacon hit him as he left the tent. He began to salivate.

'Smells pretty good, doesn't it,' he said to the pups

whimpering at his heels. 'Come on, I'll shout you.'

Luke sat under his tree and tore open the bag around one of two burgers. He gave it to the pups, who chewed it eagerly. 'Better than sheep guts, ay, Filth,' he said, biting into the other, closing his eyes and drowning in the sheer heaven of it.

He watched the showgrounds come to life. Trucks and utes and four-wheel drives rolled in until the grounds were choked with vehicles. An announcer started calling for late entries over a crackling loudspeaker.

The kid on the grey rode over with two other children, a girl and a boy, sitting behind the saddle. 'See those pups? They been eating sheep guts,' he told them proudly. 'You shoulda seen 'em puking everywhere. And that yellow one, he crapped all over the place.'

'Orr, deadly,' laughed the boy.

'Ewww,' complained the girl.

'Hey, Dingo, you riding in the draft?'

'My name's Luke.'

'You riding in the draft, Dingo Luke?'

'Depends if my ride ever gets here,' he answered. 'Do you know Bob Stockman? I'm waiting for him to get here.'

'Yeah, yeah, we know Bob, don't we?' the boy said, turning to the other two children.

'Yeah, yeah, Bob Stockman,' they chorused. 'And Paulie Stockman too.'

'I know Ted Stockman and old Frank Stockman,' said the girl.

'And Perry Stockman.'

'And One-eye Willy Stockman, him too.'

'Big family,' Luke commented.

'Oh no, they not kin, they all just stockmen!'

'Okay,' said Luke, wondering if anyone really knew Bob, his Bob.

'Hey, you can ride my dad's horses. He can't ride. He got his eye all cut up at the hospital and now he can't see straight. His horses are just tied to the truck sleeping all day.'

'Who's your dad?'

'He's *Pete* Stockman,' said the kid proudly.

'Is he an artist, by any chance?' asked Luke, beginning to feel confused.

'What?'

'Nothing.'

The man from the hospital waiting room walked up behind the kids. He had a large pair of sunglasses on and Luke could see a white patch under one of the lenses. The man slung an arm over the rump of the grey horse.

'Dad, Dingo Luke can ride your horses, get your prize money for you!'

The man nodded to Luke. 'You were at the hospital.'

Luke pointed to his plastered arm and nodded.

'You looking for a ride?' the man asked.

'Well, yeah,' said Luke. 'My ride hasn't turned up. Entries close any minute.'

'You any good? Can you handle a stallion?'

'No worries.'

'With that arm?'

Luke stopped, unsure. Not only was he reduced to one hand, but it was his left hand. 'Should be okay if he neck-reins.'

It must have been the right answer, because Pete nodded. 'Wanna ride the young ones? Go easy on 'em, just give 'em a run?'

'Yeah, yeah, for sure.'

'Go halves in the money?'

'Great. How many horses you got?'

Pete led him to a small white truck with four horses tethered to it. Luke looked over Pete's entry forms and realised he could enter two horses in the junior event as well.

'Sure, sure,' said Pete. 'Take the mare and the gelding in it. Better get your entries in quick, ay!'

Luke raced to the secretary's tent with the two pups leaping and bounding alongside him. He picked up the form and when he saw the date at the top he paused and stared at it. October thirty-first.

Sweet sixteen, hey? Happy birthday to me.

Luke messily filled out a form with his left hand and paid an extra late fee.

He walked back to the truck via the cattle yards and stopped to look in on the brumbies. The little mare looked fuller in the flanks and more comfortable already. All four horses stood close together with their ears flicking back and forth, ready to take flight at the slightest provocation.

Rusty still had the rope around his neck and Luke could see that he had cuts up the side of one front leg.

'I'll get you out of there soon, Rusty,' he said with a quiet intensity.

'Can you get that pup outta there?' demanded a voice. 'Better tie 'em both up, hey?'

Luke hopped up on the rail and saw Fang, swinging off the nostril of a large red bullock. The bullock roared and flung its head around, but Fang held on for all it was worth.

'Fang!' Luke yelled. He looked earnestly at the irate stockman. 'He's honestly not my dog!'

'Well, I'm gonna shoot it if you don't get it out of there, real quick,' the man grumbled.

The bull flung Fang clear over the rail. He landed with a yelp and scrambled to his feet. Luke pounced and dragged him away by the scruff of the neck.

'What am I going to do with you?'

Back at the truck, Pete saw them coming and opened

the hatch of a small mesh box behind the mudguard. 'Chuck it in the dog box,' he said.

Luke shoved the pup in and Pete snapped a padlock on it. He turned to Luke. 'You got some clothes to put on? We got dress regs up here, you know.'

Pete had changed into a fancy black western shirt with white piping around the yoke, tucked neatly into his jeans. His boots looked freshly polished and his hat had been dusted off.

'My friend was going to bring me some,' said Luke.

'Hey, what happened to you, Dingo Luke?' asked the little boy, still sitting on the grey horse. 'You been wrestling them buffalo up north or something?'

Luke winked at him and ran a hand over his lumpy ribs. 'Yep. Real nasty he was.' He fingered the scab on his shoulder. 'And this one was from a wild fella who tried to knife me. Before I'd even had breakfast.'

'He got you good, Dingo Luke!'

'He sure did . . . what's your name?'

'Toby!' the boy said, wheeling his horse about and raising his hat. 'Toby Stockman, and this 'ere is my horse, Greybo!'

'Of course,' laughed Luke.

'You can ride with me if you want, Buffalo Luke!'

'Sure, Toby Stockman, I'd like that.'

Pete came out from the front of the truck with some

159

jeans and a football jersey in his hands. 'These might fit you.'

'Cheers,' said Luke with relief.

Pete looked him up and down briefly, then shook his head.

'Don't ask,' said Luke.

'Don't worry, I ain't going to,' said Pete. 'You wanna give all these horses a ride, find out what they're like, see how you go one-handed?' He began to untie the black mare.

Luke pulled the jersey over his head and stepped into the jeans. They were a bit baggy, but fine. 'Sure, let's go!'

20

LUKE GAVE ALL FOUR of Pete's horses a quick ride while the ladies' event was on, and was pleasantly surprised. The black mare was soft and responsive and neck-reined well. Luke had more trouble steering the gelding with only one hand, but got along better once he tied the reins in a knot and held onto that. The stallion was wary and nervous and Luke resolved to give him a good workout before his event to settle him down. The fourth horse was an old white mare, who was a bit slow but had clearly been to a draft or two. As Luke jumped off and gave her a pat, he felt confident that he could win at least a couple of hundred dollars.

He rode over to the practice area on the black mare and helped Toby practise for the little kids' class, teaching him how to ride mirrors. They faced their horses nose to nose, and as Luke legged the mare to the left and then to the right, Toby mirrored every move with Greybo. When

Luke began to zip back and forth quickly and erratically, as a cornered steer would do, the little horse locked on beautifully.

'Now go out there and win,' Luke told Toby, as they rode over to the arena.

Toby blitzed it in the camp. He picked a small, runty black steer that moved quickly, but Greybo was all over it. Out in the arena he got two pegs and won the event. He puffed out his chest like a rooster's when he went to collect his trophy. Pete and Luke cheered madly from the sidelines.

Luke had at least another hour before his first event started. He wandered over to the tree and took his boots off. A warm breeze blew gently over him, lifting the hairs on his arms and giving him goosebumps.

He wriggled his feet down into the smooth, silty dirt and planted them, really planted them, connecting, drawing on the strength that he found in the land. He took a long, slow breath and felt it blow away the shadows of his past. He thought of iron-age warriors, with the strength of horses and the cunning of wolves, and he drew on their power. A warrior-like energy grew inside him, bold, courageous and strategic.

That's your old ones, looking after you . . .

He placed his hands together and thought of connecting, through his head, to the sky.

Ride with me again, Harry.

At Pete's truck, he untied the black mare and tightened her girth. He gave her a rub on the forehead. She was sweet, only young. He would need to take it easy on her, as Pete had said.

'All fired up?' asked Pete.

'Yep.'

Luke rode as he'd never ridden before. The feet of the little black mare seemed to connect directly with his mind, and he found he could guide her with little but a thought, as they blocked a huge, rangy Brahman that threatened to leap out of the camp. Luke kept the mare cool, sitting quiet and calmly placing her in front of the beast, driving it forward until the gate-men released it into the arena.

The beast ran fast and the mare galloped up on its flank, shouldering it around one peg, crossing over neatly behind it and then turning it back around the second peg.

'Go, Dingo Luke!' he could hear half a dozen kids yelling on the sidelines.

He steadied the mare back and brought the steer easily through the finish pegs.

Adrenaline was pumping through his body. That had

to be the fastest gate he'd ever ridden.

'Over here, Dingo Luke, over here!' Toby screamed.

Still puffing, Luke pointed the mare towards the fence where the boy and his friends sat waving and cheering madly.

'That's my dad's horse!' Toby was yelling to all his friends. 'Over here, Dingo Luke!'

As Luke approached the fence, Toby swung both his legs over the top rail and stood up. 'Closer, closer,' he said, waving his arms, and then took a flying leap onto the back of the mare, sending her into a startled canter. He waved enthusiastically to the crowd.

Outside the arena, Luke slipped out of the saddle and left the mare for Toby to walk around and cool off. He swung a leg over the gelding and found he had a very different feel: bigger, rounder, more solid on his feet. He drummed his hooves up and down excitedly and chomped at the bit.

Luke stroked the gelding's neck and soothed him back to a walk. It didn't take long to get him warmed up and working well, so he rode over to the camp, parked the horse outside and took the opportunity to watch some other riders. The gelding stood quietly as Luke sat in the saddle, folded his arms and enjoyed the event.

The level of horsemanship covered everything from people who could barely stay in the saddle to competitors on sleek, well-bred horses carving out huge scores.

As the rider before him galloped out into the arena, Luke was ushered into the camp. The gelding immediately woke up and began prancing again. Luke sat steady, eyeing the cattle. They all looked the same: grey, big, with panicky wild eyes. He got the gelding working as soon as he could, slipping it behind the first beast that wandered down the fence and hunting it to the end of the yard. The gelding pounced to the left and put in a good block.

As he blocked it for the second time, though, Filth shot out of nowhere, tail wagging.

'Oh, crikey, Filth, not now!'

Filth put his ears back and slunk about the yard with a long drooling tongue.

'*Gate!*' Luke yelled and galloped straight over the top of the pup and out into the arena, too early to get a good score. The steer bolted in a dead straight line and Luke was too far behind it to turn it.

'*Would the owner of the dog chain it up, please,*' he heard the announcer say in an annoyed voice.

Outside the arena, Luke dismounted, cursing himself for letting a stray dog ruin his run. He should have just worked straight over the top of it. When he saw the pup bolt beneath a startled horse and come gambolling towards him, he crouched down on one knee and gave a short whistle. 'Filth!'

The yellow pup sidled shamefacedly up to Luke, his tail wiggling in small apologetic movements between his back legs.

'Don't you even try looking cute,' said Luke. He grabbed Filth, shook him angrily and carried him, whimpering, back to the truck.

Pete took hold of the pup and shoved him unceremoniously into the box with Fang. Both of them howled in protest and then began growling and squabbling with each other.

'Shame,' said Pete. 'That's my most experienced horse. Thought you'd do well on him.'

'So did I,' said Luke. 'Bloody dog.'

Luke didn't connect so well with the white mare, who was headstrong and determined to do things her own way. She reminded him a bit of Chelpie back home, only she wasn't a true white. Together they did a respectable cut-out and rounded two pegs before losing control of the beast.

Back at the truck, Pete had some cold drinks and steak sandwiches. 'May as well have some lunch. Stallion event's not on until later this arvo.'

Luke tethered the mare and joined Pete on the tailgate. He looked up to the roof of the truck. 'Reckon we'd get a good view from up there?'

Pete reached up and pulled at a ladder suspended across the top of the horse crate. 'Usually do.'

Sitting on old milk crates on the roof of the truck, Pete and Luke could see across the entire grounds. Luke could see Brownie and the young brumbies in the yard, but Chocky and the colts had been moved. He scanned about but couldn't see them.

'Wonder what they've done with those other horses,' he said, mostly to himself.

'The wild ones?' asked Pete.

'Yeah, there were two yards of them. Now I can only see one.'

'They'll have 'em out the back in the chutes, getting ready for the wild horse race.'

Luke winced at the thought of the colts being chased around and roped by teams of cowboys. He tried not to think about them. 'Many stallions here?' he asked, focusing his thoughts on his chances in the next event.

'Yeah. You'll have to ride hard if you want to win that.'

The stallion was a deep claret-coloured bay, small and sporty-looking. 'Reo', his name was. He looked like a drover's horse with a set of chain hobbles buckled around his neck and a shaggy mane. He stood with a high head and alert ears that flicked back and forth. A mare was ridden past and he whinnied loudly after her.

Luke rubbed his broad, flat forehead and looked into his large eye. The horse rolled his eyeball and looked back. 'Steady, Reo.'

'He hasn't been out much,' said Pete.

Luke could tell. 'Has he worked cattle?'

'Oh yeah,' grinned Pete. 'He's a smart horse. You better hold on.'

Something about the twinkle in Pete's one good eye told Luke he was in for an interesting ride. He looked the stallion over. He was in paddock condition, with a sun-bleached coat, but Luke noticed his well-muscled hindquarters. 'Cutting horse bloodlines?'

'Mixed with a bit of Repeat,' said Pete slyly.

Luke felt his expectations suddenly rise. This horse had some of the best bloodlines in the country. 'Repeat, hey?' Repeat was a legend.

He led Reo away from the truck, the stallion prancing alongside him. Once mounted, he was over-excited, wanting to jump all over every mare he came across. 'Whoa,' soothed Luke, rubbing his neck with his plastered hand.

He took the stallion to a quiet spot away from the arena and began working him. He was fast, Luke discovered.

Probably even faster than Biyanga. The horse galloped from a standstill, reaching what felt like a hundred kilometres an hour in a split second, then slid to a halt leaving six-foot-long skid marks behind him. He was soft and super-responsive, needing barely a touch of the reins or a shift in the saddle to guide him. Luke would need to ride him with precision, he realised, or he would easily blow up.

He kept the horse quietly walking around the grounds until he heard his number called, then lined up outside the camp, waiting. The stallion's shoulders twitched and his ears flicked every time a beast moved. He was one cowy horse, all right.

A stockman motioned for him to come to the gate and, as he moved Reo up, Pete approached him on the ground. He put a hand on the stallion's bridle. 'Don't hold him too tight in the camp. He doesn't like a short rein. Just give him his head and work him with your legs. But don't let him get on top of the beast. He sometimes gets in too close.'

Luke nodded, soaking up the advice.

Pete gave Reo a slap on the neck. 'No gates yet, you could win this thing.'

The stockman opened the gate for Luke and he rode in. The cattle were tall, leggy and racy-looking. Quick, and perfect for a horse like Reo.

The stallion bounced up and down beneath him, grinding at the bit. Luke remembered Pete's advice and resisted the temptation to take up the reins. He legged him around to face the cattle and decided to pick one from the middle of the herd. He swung his feet forward, leaned back a little and felt Reo hustle backwards beneath him. Pete was right – he was a seat and legs horse. Luke centred himself and made sure he was well-balanced.

Backing off a little more to let the mob loosen up, he positioned himself to the side of his beast, waiting for it to wander to one side, then slipped in and cut it swiftly from the mob. Reo felt electrified, charged. He drummed his feet, anxious for the next command. Luke watched the steer's eye and held the stallion steady until he was sure it was going to turn that way, then let the horse spin and follow. Reo went after it like lightning, but Luke was quick to steady him, pulling him up before he got too close. A few more blocks and Luke had the beast and the horse all but line-dancing. He was having so much fun he didn't want to call for the gate.

When he did call it, the stallion whooshed after the steer as though it was on the end of a towing rope. He was like a Ferrari, roaring up on its flank and turning it nimbly around each peg, until beast, horse and rider galloped through the finishing pegs.

Luke pulled Reo up with his heart nearly pounding

out of his chest and a smile that almost split his head in half. What a horse!

He got off and led the panting stallion out of the arena. Before long, Toby and his friends were tailing them. 'You got ninety, Dingo Luke. You gonna win this thing!'

21

LUKE REACHED THE truck to find Pete and two other friends celebrating on top of it. They began drumming their feet on the roof as he approached, sending Reo careering backwards in a huge spook. 'Your shout at the pub tonight, Dingo Luke,' Pete laughed as Luke tried to regain control of the stallion.

'I haven't won it yet,' said Luke, looking up at him and smiling. Ninety was the best score he'd ever got, but a good rider could still easily knock him off.

'Yeah, you have,' said one of Pete's mates. 'Last two riders got cracked out. It's yours!'

'Five hundred bucks between us,' whooped Pete. 'We should go to the pub for a big feed, celebrate!'

'Sounds good to me,' laughed Luke. He hadn't eaten properly for days. 'Do I look eighteen?'

Pete shrugged. 'Who cares?'

Luke gave Reo a rub on the forehead. 'We'd better go

back and claim our prize money then, buddy!'

While Pete and Luke watered horses and packed gear away, Toby ran around with four colourful ribbons tied to his arm: one of his own, two places from the filly, and a big blue sash from the stallion. 'This is our best draft ever! Dingo Luke rides 'em heaps better than you, Dad!'

'You wanna go get the prize money while I load up these horses?' Pete asked Luke. 'You gotta go to the secretary's tent and give 'em your ticket.'

'Yep, sure,' said Luke. 'I just gotta use some of that money to settle some other business first. I bought some brumbies from the stock contractor.' He punched the air, stoked that he'd have money left over.

Pete pulled a face. 'What for?'

Luke shrugged. 'Just to let them go. He was going to send them to the slaughter yards.'

Pete looked baffled, but shrugged as he unlocked the box and let the pups out. They landed on the ground in a squirmy tangle of legs and tails and bounded straight over to Luke with their tongues hanging out.

Luke set off to collect his winnings from the secretary's tent with his fingers in his belt loops, a whistle on his lips and a lightness in his step. He felt taller, stronger, prouder than he ever had in his life.

He looked around at the two pups at his heels. They truly were goofy-looking with their long snouts, droopy jowls and huge fat paws. Their tails seemed too long for their bodies. And for some strange reason they seemed to utterly adore him. He bent over and gave them a pat. 'Why me?'

Filth instantly rolled on his back and piddled in the air with excitement. Fang jumped over him and got squirted. Luke looked at them with a mix of disgust, endearment and disappointment. 'Why couldn't you be blue heelers or something useful?'

'Dingo, Dingo, quick!' Toby yelled urgently, galloping up behind him and pulling Greybo to a sliding stop. 'The coppers are here, they're asking for some fella called Luke Matheson! That you?'

Sister Suzie!

Luke's eyes darted about. He saw it. A big four-wheel drive with blue-and-white checks down the side and sirens and aerials all over it. Sister Suzie in the front seat, pointing at him.

'It's the grey nurse!' shrieked Toby.

Luke looked about frantically. 'They've seen me, Toby, where do I go?'

'Jump on the back!' screamed Toby. 'I'll take you to the river. Jump on quick!'

Luke sprang up behind Toby and both he and the boy flapped their legs against the horse's sides, galloping straight for the gap between the cop car and the dagwood-dog stand.

Sister Suzie stepped out and tried to block them, waving her arms and hopping about like a soccer goalie. But Toby rode straight over the top of her, sending her leaping out of the way and crashing into a queue of hungry dagwood-dog customers. Luke turned to see Fang and Filth take flying leaps and land on her. Fang took hold of her trouser leg, growling with high-pitched puppyish rage. Filth lay on her chest and smothered her with kisses. She screamed at the police to get them off.

Luke and Toby sailed over a timber fence and headed straight for the scrub. They galloped in and out of trees and the scrub got thicker and thicker. As the showgrounds grew further and further behind them, they slowed to a walk, keeping under the cover of the trees. Soon they reached an overgrown section of the river, choked thick with pandanus and palms.

'I think we lost them,' panted Toby.

'Did you see the dogs?' laughed Luke.

'Yeah, that pup slobbered all over her!'

They rode for a little while longer and then Luke slipped off the horse and looked back behind him.

He gave a short whistle.

The bush was quiet.

Luke stood and waited, hopeful.

There was a rustle, and first Fang, then Filth, came gambolling along the track. Luke knelt on one knee and held his arms out. They dived into his lap and wiggled excitedly, puffing and slobbering profusely.

'I think them pups wanna be yours,' said Toby.

'I reckon there's no getting around it now,' said Luke, jerking his chin away from an enthusiastic tongue. 'Pwah, have to change their diet though. No more offal for you, matey,' he said, pushing Filth away. 'What about you? You going back?'

'I ain't going near them coppers,' said Toby.

Luke wondered why but said nothing.

'Don't ask,' said Toby.

'Don't worry,' said Luke, shaking his head. 'I ain't gonna. But what about your dad?'

'We know how to find each other out here, no worries,' said Toby. 'And if we run into a croc, you can wrestle him, like you did that buffalo.'

'Are there crocs in this river?'

'Prob'ly not.'

'That means maybe yes.'

'Yeah, but what are the chances?' said the kid. 'That's what Dad always says.'

'Yeah, what are the chances,' agreed Luke.

They headed back along the river. When the pups got tired, Luke scooped them up and put them in the saddlebags. Toby broke tree branches and arranged various stones as they went, leaving a trail for Pete.

22

THE SUN WAS SETTING by the time they found the spot where Luke had camped with Tyson and Tex. When they reached the causeway, Luke quickly found the swag and his pack. They had been rolled up and placed under some bushes. Next to them was a bag of groceries and a handline with a few spare lures.

'Bob's been here,' said Luke, pushing Filth's nose out of the bag. 'Look, he left us some tucker.' He turned to Toby. 'You any good at fishing?'

'Never tried,' said Toby, jumping down from Greybo and unbuckling his saddle.

'Don't worry. I'm an expert. I'll catch us a big barra!' said Luke. 'There's a big horse paddock behind all those trees,' said Luke. 'Let the horse go out there for a pick if you want.' He showed Toby how to use a stirrup leather for hobbles.

Toby led the horse through the river and disappeared.

Meanwhile, Luke inspected the lures. There were a few different types. He decided to just go for the biggest one. Surely that would catch the biggest fish. Pulling a few metres of line off the reel, he threw the lure into the water and tied the other end to a tree branch.

'That oughta do it,' he mumbled to himself, walking back to the bag of groceries. 'No need to stand around holding it all night.'

There were tins of soup and some crackers. He rummaged through his pack and felt around for a box of matches, then collected some kindling to start a fire. A fat locust landed in his shoulder and clung on with its barbed legs. Crickets chirruped and birds argued with each other as the sun dipped below the horizon. Cane toads smashed about in the bushes. Filth started leaping in after them.

'Don't go eating one of those or you'll be sorry,' Luke said.

He struck a match and watched the fire crackle to life. Toby came back and sat next to him, wrapping his arms around his knees. He'd gone a bit quiet since the sun started setting. Fang nuzzled under his arm and the boy let him crawl onto his lap.

'You all right there, little stockman?'

'Yeah, me and Dad camp out all the time.'

Toby started rocking back and forth and looking

around at the darkening trees and water. Luke thought of Chocky and the way he looked after Rusty.

'I got a real good swag. You can sleep in it if you want, and I'll sleep right next to you, just until your dad comes. He won't be long.'

'Yeah, he'll be coming soon,' said the kid, nodding and looking into the fire.

Luke dragged the end of a big branch over and laid it on the flames, then opened the box of crackers and offered it to Toby, who shook his head.

'Reckon there really would be any salties?' Toby asked.

'Probably not.'

'That means maybe yes.'

'Yeah, but what are the chances?' grinned Luke.

There was a huge splashing sound and both Luke and Toby jumped out of their skins. Filth and Fang leapt up and began yapping excitedly at the river.

'What was that?' Toby ran to Luke and threw his arms around his waist.

'It's my line!' gasped Luke. 'It must be huge.'

'You caught a croc, Dingo Luke!' screamed Toby, backing away from the water.

'A croc?'

The taut, jerking line was nearly snapping the branch off the tree. Fang hurled himself into the river with a mighty growl and disappeared under the surface, reappearing a few seconds later. He shook the water out of his ears and began growling and yapping again, swimming in circles.

'Fang! Get out of there, you idiot!' yelled Luke.

Whatever it was, it was the size of a large dog, maybe even a small horse. A *croc*?

Luke wasn't taking any chances. He ran away from the river and caught up with Toby. Filth ran at his heels, barking and yapping like mad.

'Do you really reckon it's a croc?' Luke stared in vain through the trees. 'Hope Fang hasn't been eaten!'

Toby clamped his arms around Luke's waist again and peered around from behind him. 'See it rolling?' he whispered. 'That's its death roll. It wants to take you under the water and roll you around until your arms fall off. Then he wants to ram you under a rock until you rot and then he can eat your guts out!'

'Whoa,' said Luke.

'Let's camp up in the hills,' whispered Toby.

'What about all our food and the swag?'

'You go an' get them.'

'Are crocs scared of fire?'

'Yeah, yeah, you'll be right,' said Toby, loosening his grip on Luke's waist. 'Just go real quiet. I'll wait here and look after the pup.'

The monster in the river kept jerking and thrashing about in the water, sending waves a metre high all around it and bending the tree branch to snapping point.

'Reckon we really need our stuff?' asked Luke. 'That thing looks real angry to me.'

A wave of light arced over the river and the sound of tyres over gravel rolled up behind them.

'Quick, quick, it's the cops!' squeaked Toby, jumping up and down. 'We got to run to the hills!' He tugged urgently at Luke's arm. Fang shot out of the water and together the two pups began barking at the car with puppyish fury.

Luke squinted into the headlights. He could see no sirens or aerials. The car had low-set round lights, like those on an HQ ute.

'It's Bob!' yelled Luke. 'Bob!' He waved his arms euphorically and scruffed Toby on the head. 'It's okay, Toby. It's a mate of mine!'

Toby went quiet and slid behind Luke, without letting go of his waist. Luke walked over to the car, dragging the boy behind him. 'I thought you knew Bob Stockman?'

'Bob Stockman,' whispered Toby. 'Who's that?'

'You know, Paulie and Frank and all that mob,' said Luke, twisting around and trying to detach the boy's arms. 'One-eyed Willy!'

'A one-eyed what?'

Luke just shook his head. When he reached the driver's side window, he realised there was another car pulling up behind.

'Tyson!' yelled Luke. 'Quick, we caught a big croc! It's tied to a tree!'

The second car came to a stop and Luke watched a big springy-haired silhouette step out.

'What's that?' Tyson asked.

'We caught a crocodile. It's in the water, tied to a tree!'

'What are you talking about?' said Tyson, pushing past Luke and walking down to the river. Bob rolled his ute down onto the causeway and shone the headlights on the splashes that were still erupting from the river. Something silvery flapped in the light.

Tyson turned to Luke. '*What* did you say it was?'

'Ummm,' said Luke, gingerly taking a few steps closer. 'We weren't exactly sure.'

Tyson waded into the water and seized the line. He pulled a knife from his back pocket, cut the line from the tree, and began hauling a huge ugly fish towards the bank.

'Geez, give me a hand, Luke,' he grunted, the line winding tightly around his hands. 'Grab a big thick stick!'

Luke pounced on a thick branch and waded through the river to Tyson.

'Wrap the line round it,' said Tyson, grimacing.

Luke began winding the stick around and around the line until it was well and truly secured. Then Tyson unwound his hand and shook it out, cursing under his breath. 'You bring her in, big fulla,' he said to Luke. 'She's all yours.'

Luke hung onto the wood with his one good hand; his broken arm had no strength at all. He staggered backwards into the knee-deep water. The fish yanked at his arm, lunging from side to side. 'Come and help me, Toby,' he yelled, planting his feet into a pile of pebbles. 'It's your fish too!'

Toby needed no second invitation. He leapt into the water and, with his arms over the top of Luke's, began tugging at the fish, hauling it up and over the riverbank until it lay flapping on the dirt, with Fang and Filth darting back and forth and snapping at it.

'Where'd the wolves come from?' asked Bob.

'Mate, that is without a doubt the biggest barra I ever saw in my life!' said Tyson, dripping wet, his hands on his hips. 'That is one big mother of a barramundi.'

Luke stood proudly looking at his catch, the line still in his hand.

Luke Matheson. Man of steel. Big hunter!

'She's a big breeder. You gonna keep her or let her go?' asked Bob, staring down at the fish with his hands in his pockets.

'Up to you, Luke,' said Tyson.

'We got anything else to eat?' asked Luke.

'Dry crackers,' said Tyson.

'Let's eat it, let's eat it!' sang Toby, suddenly getting over his shyness. 'It's my fish too. Let's eat it!'

Tyson grinned. 'I was hoping you'd say that.'

He showed the boys how to bleed, gut and scale the fish, and then they built the fire up until they had plenty of hot ashes.

'So where've you been?' Luke asked Bob as they mounded the coals up over the fish.

Bob and Tyson looked at each other with sheepish grins.

'Helping the coppers. They've been asking after you,' said Bob.

'Been driving around all day, looking for you,' said Tyson.

'Yeah, everywhere: Burketown, Normanton, Karumba,' chuckled Bob. 'It was a lovely drive.'

The two men began giggling like a pair of schoolgirls. 'Them coppers gave us nice pub meals for helping 'em, too. Too bad we couldn't find you, ay.'

'Not till the end of the day, anyway,' said Tyson. 'We told the coppers you wouldn't be at the draft, but they wouldn't listen. More we told 'em not to, the more they wanted to go there. Didn't you see us in the back of the cop car? The grey nurse was goin' off her rocker.'

'That was some fancy riding you did, kid,' said Bob to Toby. 'Jumping over the big fence like that and rescuing Luke.'

Toby smiled shyly. 'I won the kids' draft, too. I got a trophy.'

'I'm not surprised,' said Tyson. 'Where'd you learn to ride like that?'

'We told your dad where you'd be,' Bob said. 'He's just taking the horses home, then he's gonna meet us down here.'

The huge barramundi fed all of them, plus the dogs. Pete joined them just as Luke and Toby pulled it out of the coals. 'Look what we caught, Dad!' Toby yelled to him. 'Come and look. Me and Dingo Luke pulled it in! He's heaps better at fishing than you, Dad!'

Pete roughed his son's hair good-naturedly. 'That's cos he's got more eyes than me, boy!'

They sat cross-legged in the glow of the fire, shadows cast over their faces, laughing and swapping stories as they recalled the day's adventures, eating juicy chunks of the huge fish steaming in the crumpled silver foil.

Pete told Luke that he had tried to collect the winnings, but the secretary wouldn't hand them over. He had paid the contractor for the brumbies with his own money. The man thought Luke had skipped out on him and sold them to Pete for a fifty. Luke was overjoyed – although now that he 'owned' them, he knew he'd spend the entire night agonising over what to do with them. 'I promise I'll pay you back,' he told Pete.

As they ran out of stories and settled to watching the fire in contented silence, Tyson moved over and sat by Luke. 'So, what are you gonna do now, Luke? You gonna live up here on the river your whole life?'

'Or are you gonna go back home and give Lawson a chance?' put in Bob.

Luke took a while to answer. He needed to know something first. Looking directly at Bob, he asked, 'Did he send you after me? When you found me at the truckstop that morning, did Lawson send you?'

Bob paused before answering. 'Course he did,' he said softly.

And with those few small words, Luke felt an immense pulling in his gut, like nothing he'd ever felt before: for his people, for his river, for the huge coachwood trees and the grassy flats that snaked alongside them, linking all the properties and people together like a long green highway.

Lawson, Annie, the smell of fresh pine shavings in the stables. It was where Luke belonged and he suddenly ached for it.

He wanted to run his hands up Legsy's neck and scratch him between the ears. He wanted to eat Sunday breakfasts on the verandah. He wanted to rumble with Tom. And he wanted an apprenticeship, a job. He knew more than anything that he wanted to be a farrier.

That's what he needed, he realised: a good job, a good horse, and a good strong mob. He'd worked it out. He remembered Harry: what he wouldn't give to hear his rusty old voice and his boots shuffling down the stable aisle.

And he thought of Jess. He wasn't going to wait until he just ran into her at some horse event. They had something worth sharing. Something that connected them.

The way you have with these horses. You've got dream there, you and this Jess girl.

Somehow, he knew, she was a part of the equation.

Early the next morning, Toby and Tyson went looking for turtles. They came back with three long-necks and buried them on their backs in the hot coals and ash. Half an hour later, Tyson pulled off the breastplates and scooped out the meat. Luke tried some. It was unusual, and not at all like chicken as he had been told.

'I want to go and get those brumbies,' Luke said, as he sat next to Bob.

'What are you gonna do with a mob of wild horses?' asked Bob.

'I just want to let them go. Otherwise they'll go to the knackery. I can't just leave them there.'

'They'll only be rounded back up. Word is there'll be another big cull soon. Their numbers are getting too big again.'

'A cull?'

'They'll be heli-mustered, transported for days, train, then truck. They'll be killed for human consumption. Closest abattoir licenced for human-consumption horses is Caboolture – days away. They don't travel well, the wild ones. Better off letting 'em go to the local knackery, I reckon.'

Luke's heart sank. 'Yeah, you're right,' he admitted. 'What am I gonna do with a mob of wild horses? I don't even know if I have a home to go to.'

'You better go find out, ay,' suggested Bob.

23

'LAWSON.'

There was silence on the other end of the phone.

'It's Luke.'

'Where are you?'

'Up in the Gulf.'

'What do you want?'

Luke was tempted to slam the phone straight back down into the receiver, but he sucked it up. 'I want a job.'

There was silence again. Luke tried to imagine Lawson's face.

'Don't worry about it. I shouldn't have rung.' Luke pulled the phone from his ear and had it halfway to the cradle when he heard Lawson speak. 'Wait.'

The phone made muffled noises as Lawson covered the receiver. He spoke to someone else and excused himself. Then his voice became clear again. 'What?'

'A job,' said Luke. 'I want a job.'

He heard Lawson exhale into the phone.

Further down the road, Sister Suzie's white four-wheel drive turned in to the hospital grounds. Toby popped out from behind some bushes and pointed urgently at the vehicle.

Luke nodded at him. He kept his head down and tried to look inconspicuous. Pete's football jersey was good camouflage. They were all football-mad around here — didn't seem to matter what team or code.

'What sort of job you after?' asked Lawson, sounding cautious.

'I want to be a farrier.'

Again, Lawson didn't answer.

There was a noisy clatter as a handful of stones hit the glass wall of the phone booth. Luke looked up just in time to see a cop walking to his car. It figured that the only phone booth in town had to be right outside the police station.

'Sorry about . . . you know, hitting you,' said Luke. 'I was out of line.'

'Yeah, I didn't expect that from you,' said Lawson.

'I didn't expect it either. I was out of control.'

'I was so determined not to fight with Ryan and then you bloody hit me.'

This wasn't going to be a quick kiss-and-make-up, Luke could tell. 'Sorry,' he repeated.

'That was my father's funeral,' said Lawson, sounding angry, 'his wake.'

Luke's face burned with shame. 'I'm sorry.' It sounded woefully inadequate, but he didn't know what else to say.

'Yeah, whatever,' Lawson sniffed.

'So . . .'

'What?'

'So, can I have a job?'

'Come back and we'll talk about it.'

Luke tightened his jaw . . . Lawson's offer was equally an invitation back home and an attempt to boss him around. But he wasn't a foster kid anymore and he needed to get that through to Lawson. He had said sorry and he meant it, but he wasn't going to let Lawson tell him what to do – not unless he was paying to. 'If I come back, it'll be on my own terms.'

'Don't come back then,' said Lawson. 'You ring me asking for a job, and then tell me you want to state your own terms?'

'I don't want to state the terms of the job, I . . .'

'You're not family. I don't owe you anything, kid.'

Lawson's words stung. It was a blunt reminder. Luke wasn't a Blake, and never would be. He was wasting his time. He felt suddenly angry, frustrated.

'You've got no parents now either, Lawson.' It was a

low blow but Luke didn't care. 'Annie and Ryan, they're not Blakes either. You're just like me now, some mongrel-bred part of the mix.' He slammed down the phone, getting in before Lawson could.

Then he stood in the phone booth fighting the urge to smash his fist through the glass. He could have yelled until he was hoarse. He'd done it again. Blown everything.

Outside the booth, he heard tyres on gravel, rolling slowly. Cops. They were sussing him out. Luke slouched into himself and sank to the ground with his hands over his head.

From over the road, Pete called loudly. 'Hey, anyone know where the hospital is?'

The cop outside the booth answered. 'It's just over there, same place as always.'

'Where's that?'

'Right there. Up the road.'

'Oh, sorry, officer. Can't see. Got my eyes all cut up and I can't see nothin'.'

'Through the gate there.'

'You couldn't help me, could you? Don't want to get hit by a car.'

The phone booth door slid open and a small hand pulled gently at Luke's arm. 'Come on, Dingo Luke,' whispered Toby. 'We gotta go, cops everywhere.'

They hopped through backyards until they could make a break for the creek. Then they ran until they found Bob in his ute, waiting for them a couple of kays out of town.

'Can we go past the showgrounds?' asked Luke. 'I want to see my brumbies.'

'*Your* brumbies?' Bob raised his sunnies and looked at him. 'You still haven't worked out what you're gonna do?'

'I can't just leave them there. They'll get dogged.'

'They'll get dogged anyway, bro,' said Bob. 'You heard what I said: big cull coming up.'

'I've got to at least give them a chance.'

'A chance at what?'

Luke sighed. Bob was right. They had no chance. He thought of Rusty, slammed up against the brown mare, whinnying and snapping his gums. Then he imagined him being heli-mustered again, or shot and left wounded for dingos to finish off. He knew he should just leave him, but he couldn't. 'Can we just do a drive-by?'

Bob groaned, did a U-turn and headed towards the showgrounds. 'You better get down – if there's cops there they'll pull me up for sure.' He glanced across the front of the ute. 'You too, Toby.'

Luke curled onto the floor of the ute and Toby lay down on the front seat. After a while Luke felt the vehicle slow and turn. He heard gravel under the tyres and cattle bellowing in the distance, truck engines and people yelling.

'Cops are here.' Bob immediately put the ute into reverse. Luke poked his head up and scanned around. Two uniformed police were walking along the road.

'Stay down,' growled Bob.

'You're leaving!'

'Course I'm leaving. You want them gubbas to take you back in?'

'What about the brumbies?' Luke shot his head above the dashboard. Behind the cars and trucks, the yards still bustled with livestock. He caught a quick glimpse of some horses, all ears and swishing tails, brown and red and black, still struggling against their surrounds. And then they were gone. Bob backed straight out of the front gate and onto the highway.

'Lawson give you a job?' asked Bob as he put the ute into top gear.

'Nup.'

Bob gave a fleeting frown, as if surprised. 'So what are you doing? You going back?'

Luke didn't answer.

'I'm going back to the crossing to get my gear, then

I'm leaving.' Bob lifted his sunnies off his nose and turned to him. 'They're your mob, Luke. You're a big boy now, a man. You gotta look after them.'

'I can't do that without a job.'

'So go and get one.'

Back at the crossing, Luke shoved his pitifully few belongings into his pack, hoisted it onto his shoulder and stood looking at the river. As he waded through the water, something inside him crossed over. He wasn't the same person he had been when he first came to this river. He would be all right on his own now. He reached the other side, stopped and looked back. It flowed slowly and serenely, turquoise-blue and achingly beautiful.

'Moonstone Crossing, I'll call you,' he said, 'because you gave me beautiful dreams.'

As the red hills rolled by, Luke sat in the front of the ute and thought of the brumbies. Maybe some of them would survive the big cull, join other survivors and build up new herds. They would find their place within the mob. As for *his* brumbies, Brownie, Rusty and the fillies, there was no mob out in the hills to look after them anymore. Chocky and the other colts were now the property of a rodeo contractor. As for the old red stallion, Luke could only guess that something awful had happened to him. And he knew the moment Brownie lay down to foal, the wild dogs would be all over her. It would be kinder to let her be destroyed humanely. And Rusty, did he ever have a chance?

Luke laid his head back against the seat and let the soothing voice float out of the stereo and wrap around his soul. For the first time in a long while he allowed himself to think of his foster father from years ago: his swinging fists, his dark, ugly nature, and the damage he had done. Luke ran his hands over his ribs and wished he could forget what he even looked like.

He spun around and peered through the back window to check on the two pups and groaned. Filth was heaving something horrible all over Bob's saddle. Luke had buried the fish guts away from the camp so the pups couldn't get at them, but they must have dug them up.

Bob sang quietly beside him.

Roads through many faiths / the journey's not unknown / all go to one place / they take my spirit home.

A roadside servo was the first stop to welcome them back to Mount Isa.

'Sure this is what you want?' asked Bob.

Luke nodded. 'Just let me out up here.'

Bob leaned across the bench seat as Luke released his seatbelt. He held out his hand. 'See you round, ay, bro?'

'You bet,' said Luke, giving it a shake that he hoped conveyed the gratitude and respect he felt. He looked Bob in the eye. 'Thanks.'

He whistled up the pups, and set off on foot towards Mount Isa.

24

LUKE WALKED ALONG the road, dust-caked suburban sprawl on one side of him and a huge copper mine on the other. Filth and Fang bitterly resented the ropes around their necks and had to be dragged all the way.

Closer to town he came across a large saddlery, a small art gallery, an op shop and a fancy-looking cafe with people sipping lattes and forking salads. When he reached the pub in the centre of town, he sat on a public seat outside and took a breather.

A job: somehow he had to find one without getting involved with Centrelink. He looked down the road at the huge smokestacks towering over the mine and wondered where the head office might be. He'd heard that mining jobs paid great money, but how could he apply for a job without any sort of reference or résumé, let alone any ID?

He looked at the cars angle-parked along the kerb. Big white four-wheel drives, most of them, with government number plates. Or big utes. Small sedans wouldn't last long on the rough roads out here. A four-wheel drive cruiser rolled into an empty spot and two men in dirty hats got out. Luke watched them walk to the front door of the pub and disappear inside. Those were the sort of people he should ask. Ringers.

It was early afternoon. The pub was quiet. He tied the pups to the seat and decided to give it a go.

A waft of cool deodorised air hit him in the face as he pulled the big-handled doors open. *Ch-ching* pokie noises, clinking glass, quiet murmurs of conversation interspersed with outbreaks of laughter. It was a large pub, but almost empty.

A six-foot-six bouncer in a bow tie stood glaring down at him. 'Got ID, mate?'

Luke looked up at him. 'You got to be kidding me.'

The bouncer shrugged an enormous shoulder.

'I've just got to talk to those blokes over there.' Luke pointed at the ringers.

'Hey, Mac, you know this bloke?'

A man in his sixties looked up from under his hat. He wore a spotless collared shirt and was freshly shaven. He gave Luke no more than a second's glance and then turned back to his associate without answering.

The bouncer pointed to the door.

'I'll be real quick,' said Luke. 'Please.'

The hulking man stepped in front of Luke and folded his arms across his chest. 'I don't think they want to be interrupted.' Behind him, the men took long swallows of beer and continued talking.

Luke backed out of the doorway then turned and walked back to the bench seat, only to find it occupied by two women and several noisy kids, all yelling and arguing over Filth and Fang. He dragged the pups across the road and plonked himself on the edge of a raised garden bed. Through the tinted windows of the pub he could see the two men talking. He'd been wrong; they couldn't be ringers. Cattle barons, more like it.

The daylight began to fade. Luke still sat, staring into the pub. It had filled with more people and the rise and fall of voices overflowed into the street. A woman from the cafe came out and gave a bowl of water to the dogs. People passed him, many looking worse off than he. Aboriginal people, heaps of them, suddenly filled the streets. A woman with a heavily bruised face stalked along with several other women in single file behind her, small children cradled in their arms. The men were unshaven, angry-looking. They weren't like Tyson or Bob or Pete. They didn't look him in the eye or acknowledge him; somehow they seemed utterly unapproachable. Fang growled at almost every person who went past.

'Money day,' a woman said, as she walked toward

him. She was a big woman, dressed in golden scarves like a gypsy. Her hips, wrapped in a tasselled red sarong, swung from side to side as she walked. She looked Luke over lightning-quick. 'First night in the Isa?'

Luke nodded, feeling annoyed by his inability to look a bit more confident. He tried to relax his arms and not clutch his pack quite so tightly. He felt Fang's chest rumble on his foot.

'You don't want to sleep on these streets tonight,' the woman said, strutting past, 'not even with those ferocious guard dogs.'

'I'm looking for a job,' he called after her.

She looked back over her shoulder. 'Try Centrelink.'

'I can't.' Luke got up and ran after her, and to his immense relief she stopped and turned.

He stared at her and she stared back with that same blend of tenderness and bossiness that he had always seen in Annie's face. She would help him, he could tell. 'You know anywhere I could stay for the night?'

The woman looked him over some more, huffed, looked at her watch and then fumbled in her handbag. She pulled out some keys and turned back in the direction she had come from. 'Twenty bucks a night. The dogs stay outside and you clean up their shit. Be up and out by eight-thirty in the morning, and don't come back until five.'

When they reached the small art gallery, she unlocked the door and flicked on the lights. Inside, the walls and the ceiling were painted matte black and paintings of assorted styles hung everywhere. Luke took a wriggling pup in each arm as she led him past a small sales counter at the back of the studio and through a doorway into a small kitchenette. Under an enormous amount of debris was a couch.

'I stay here when I'm feeling creative,' the woman said, pulling at a mound of calico and piling it on the floor. 'Or when my husband's got the shits. I spilled a whole can of red paint over the floor at home the other day – he didn't like that much.'

Luke faked a laugh.

'Just chuck that stuff on the floor. The toilet's outside.' She looked at Filth and Fang, tucked under his arms. 'And so are the dingos. Don't lock yourself out – it's a deadlock and I'm not giving you a key.'

Luke tossed the pups out the back door into a small courtyard and reached into his pocket for his wallet.

'Fix me up tomorrow.' She glanced at her watch again. 'I gotta go. There's some half-dead lasagne in the fridge if your dogs are hungry. Don't let them near any of my art, or I'll hunt you down and kill you. I'm Talia, by the way.'

Luke stared up at the black ceiling. He wouldn't sleep here, he knew. The place was so unfamiliar after sleeping under a wide open sky – it was like wrapping a cold wet blanket around his already freezing body. But it was better than being out on the streets. He could already hear drunken voices.

He reached for the moonstone and found a bare throat, patted the front of his chest and pulled the collar of his jersey up. He ripped the shirt off. 'Where's my moonstone?'

Maybe he had put it in his pack without thinking; he grabbed it and tore it open. He scooped out the old socks, knife, maps, dried-out mandarin skins and greasy burger wrappers, threw it all on the floor and turned the pack inside out. Shook it, flung it around, slapped it against the wall. Then he hurled it across the kitchenette and watched it land on a pile of unwashed plates. A glass fell off the sink and smashed on the floor.

'Damn it,' he yelled, *damn everything!*'

Luke threw himself backwards onto the couch and put his hands over his face. 'It was all I had,' he groaned through his fingers.

His last connection to Coachwood Crossing was gone. He pulled his hands away from his face and let them hang limp down by his sides. He stared at the ceiling for a while, then rolled his head and stared out into the studio.

There was a telephone among the clutter on the sales desk. He could ring Jess and talk to her, ask how Annie was going, who was riding Legsy now, if any of the mares had foaled yet. It might help fill this empty gaping cavern in his chest. He closed his eyes and thought of her voice. Imagined it on the other end of the phone, making him laugh.

But a wave of hollow loss forced his eyes open again. He couldn't think of Jess without seeing the green river flats and the dense line of trees running along banks, without feeling a gentler sun on his skin and smelling freshly cut clover. He breathed deeply. Nope. It did him no good to think about anyone from Coachwood Crossing. He walked out to the studio.

There were a lot of touristy dot paintings in gaudy kindergarten colours, some funky fat witchetty grub pictures, bark paintings and hand stencils, all by different artists. But the huge contemporary paintings along the northern wall took his breath away. They were unbelievably intricate and reflected the greens, ochres and browns of the local country. He could see the spinifex, the chestnut-red boulders and golden grass, chalk-white tree bark; all in soft, irregular shapes with rivers of dots flowing between them. He could imagine the brumbies running through the painting and had an overwhelming urge to put his palms out and place them flat on the canvas so he could feel the earth.

At eight-thirty the next morning, Luke left a twenty-dollar note on the sales desk and let himself out through the back door.

At the local shopping centre, he washed down a couple of bananas with a can of no-name cola and looked through his wallet. It was such a bummer that he hadn't collected his winnings. All he had was a paltry ten bucks.

He needed a job, quickly. He tried to make himself look half-decent in the shopping centre toilets, washing his face, straightening out Pete's rugby jersey and combing his fingers through his hair. He rubbed a finger over his teeth, took one last glance in the mirror and hoped his grubby appearance would at least make him look like he'd been working hard.

Then he walked back out to the hot, dry streets. He would ask every station man that he saw if they knew of any work. He wouldn't stop until he found something.

Approaching people got easier after he had done it a few times. He waited outside a farm supply store and accosted the stockmen as they got out of their cars. After a while, he just asked everyone – women, children, old men, young men, black, white. Someone would have to know of something.

'Hi, mate. I'm looking for work – do you know if there's anything around?'

'I'm on the hunt for some work . . . Okay.'

'Don't know of any work going, do you, mate?'

'Hi, my name's Luke.' Quick nod. 'I'm trying to find some work.'

He collected a few phone numbers of people who might have something and found a phone box, but they all came to a dead end. He got plenty of head-scratching, thoughtful looks, best wishes, even semi-interviews, but by the time the store closed its gates at five, nothing had come up and he was left sitting in the gutter with an empty stomach and nowhere to go.

Talia unlocked the studio door and let him in. 'Don't interrupt me, I'm having an epiphany,' she said as she locked it behind him and walked to a large canvas lying flat on a table.

Luke went out the back door and held out his arms for the pups. They jumped up and lavished him with lasagne-scented kisses. 'Smells like you guys had a better feed than me,' he said, rubbing their backs.

'I fed them – they were driving me nuts. They've been crying all day,' said Talia from behind him.

Luke sniffed them again. They smelled like flowers.

'I washed them too, they stank,' said Talia. 'The yellow one loved it, but the black one tried to bite me.'

'Sorry, they're a bit feral.'

'Anyway, stop interrupting me.' Talia walked back inside.

Luke sat with his feet on the couch for hours, watching Talia work. It was almost hypnotic to see a large canvas of red swirls come to life under the careful strokes of her brushes. She hummed a tune from a children's television show as she worked. *Tobeee, Tobeee, everybody loves Tobeee* . . .

'I don't have any more money to pay you,' he said.

'Shh,' she hissed.

'But I can pay you back when—'

'Shut up or get out!'

He shut up, rolled over on the couch and drifted in and out of sleep. When he woke in the morning she was gone and the canvas was finished. It was extraordinary – fiery and swirly, with eyes in it.

There was half a loaf of stale white bread on the kitchen sink. He ate most of it and made a cup of tea. Outside, he crouched down and ran his hands over the dogs' big bony heads. 'I can't take you with me, guys. But I think Talia likes you and she'll take good care of you.'

Filth let out a loud whine and leapt at him. 'Don't make it any harder,' Luke whispered. 'There's nothing else I can do. I just need a hand until I can find a job, then maybe I can come back and get you.'

It wouldn't be too bad. No worse than staying here and scabbing off a total stranger. The department of community services would probably find some hostel or somewhere he could stay. He looked around for something to tether the pups to and found a pipe running down the side of the toilet building. He gave Filth and Fang a last pat, slung his pack onto his shoulder and walked out onto the street, trying to ignore the yelps.

25

HE FOUND A public phone in town with a battered yellow block of pissed-on pages. An old man in a beanie sat staring at him from a nearby bench. 'It's broken, ay,' he mumbled.

'I was looking for the phone book,' said Luke. 'Do you know where Centrelink is?'

'It's broken,' the man mumbled again and then proceeded to tell Luke what he thought of all Centrelink employees.

Luke looked around for someone else to ask.

'Got a dollar?' the man asked.

Luke fumbled in his pockets and took out his last few goldies. 'If I'm gonna be broke, I may as well be stony broke.' He let them drop into the man's gnarly old hand and set off to find Centrelink. It wasn't a huge town – he'd find it sooner or later. As soon as they looked up his details they'd find out he was a missing person.

A car on the other side of the road honked. Luke looked up briefly. It was a Landcruiser ute, one of hundreds around here. Nothing to do with him. He put his head down and kept walking. It honked again and he ignored it.

'Luke.'

It was a man's voice, a Coachwood Crossing voice. He'd know it anywhere. Luke spun around. On the other side of the road, a man in his thirties, tall, with a big hat and big boots, closed the door of the ute and began walking across the road.

Luke could barely believe his eyes. 'Lawson?'

Lawson walked straight at him, stopping a couple of metres away with his hands in his pockets, running his eyes over him.

Luke felt instantly self-conscious. His clothes were filthy and ill-fitting. He must look like hell.

'Hey,' said Lawson.

Luke nodded a greeting, while his mind tried to adjust. What did Lawson want? What was he doing here?

'How you been?' asked Lawson, his eyes resting momentarily on Luke's plastered arm.

'All right, I s'pose.'

Strange silence.

'Want to talk?'

'About what?'

Lawson put his hands in his back pockets and shrugged. 'Everything.'

Luke's head spun. He had just shut off all hope of ever making Coachwood Crossing his home again. He was walking in another direction. And now, here was Lawson, standing right in front of him, asking him to open it all back up.

'Come and have a beer,' said Lawson, tilting his head towards the pub over the road and looking at his watch. 'Not quite beer o'clock yet, but we could call ourselves shift workers for the morning.'

'Bouncer in that pub already kicked me out.'

'He won't if you're with me,' said Lawson. 'Come on.' He began to cross the road and looked back to see if Luke was coming.

Luke followed cautiously and Lawson waited for him to catch up. They walked side by side, both with their hands in their pockets.

In a quiet courtyard out the back, Lawson put two beers on the table and sat down. Luke left his untouched and waited for Lawson to speak, wondering what the hell was worth a three-day drive to come and talk about.

Lawson stared into his glass and picked at the calluses on his fingers. 'Been thinking about what you said,' he muttered after a while. 'You're right, Harry was the only family I had. Feel like a part of myself's died.'

Luke stayed quiet.

Lawson kept talking. 'I'll never forget when he taught me to break in my first horse.' He smiled into his beer. 'Dusty. He was a brumby. A herd-bound little fella, had the strongest sense of his mob. Harry made me do all the groundwork over and over, wouldn't let me even think of getting on him till I had his complete respect on the ground. He reckoned I'd never ever have a partnership with him unless I established myself as the leader.' Lawson laughed. 'Imagine trying to teach that to a thirteen-year-old kid. God, I just wanted to get on him and ride the buck out of him.'

Luke couldn't help a small laugh. That was just so Lawson.

'He was right, though,' said Lawson. 'Sometimes if you want respect, you do have to step up, be a leader.'

'So did the horse buck?'

'Nup.' Lawson looked up and grinned. 'I was so pissed off; my first breaker and barely a bloody pigroot. Where was the glory in that?' He shook his head. 'Geez, that little brumby turned out to be a good horse, though.'

'That why you went and rode rodeo for a while?'

'Yeah. The old man's way was no bloody fun.' Lawson laughed. 'I left home at fifteen and rode steers and broncs for a few years, bulls when I turned eighteen. Harry was absolutely disgusted with me.'

Luke ran his hand through his hair and thought of Harry. He was such a brilliant old fella. Luke couldn't imagine being so lucky as to have him as a real father, to be brought up with all that knowledge and guidance at your fingertips, every day in the round yards and in the stables. The almost-four years he'd had with Harry had been the best of his life. Lawson had had thirty years of it.

'First horse I ever broke in with Harry was a filly. I got tossed halfway across the property,' said Luke. 'Landed outside the rails.'

'Lucky bastard,' grinned Lawson.

'I forgot to take my spurs off.'

Lawson roared with laughter. 'The old man woulda seen them, too.'

Luke laughed with him. 'Yeah, he did, but he let me get on and make my own mistakes. I never did it again.'

'I bet you didn't,' chuckled Lawson. He downed the last of his beer and sat quiet for a while.

Luke looked at Lawson's face. It was so much like Harry's: the big nose, the heavy-set jaw. He had a thick head of black hair, though. Harry was a bald old codger.

'You weren't the first foster kid we ever had come to live with us,' said Lawson.

'I know.'

'We had a few of them when I was growing up. The old man thought they would be good friends for us, you know, because we lived a long way out of town.' Lawson shook his head. 'But I hated it. I had to share everything with them, my home, my room, my father. I never asked for any of them.'

Luke began to feel small again.

'But you were different,' said Lawson. 'You always showed me some respect. You never cut in between me and the old man.'

'You weren't upset that he asked me to ride Biyanga?'

Lawson looked Luke in the eye and shook his head. 'He saw you as a real mate and I respected that. If he wanted you to ride Biyanga, then that was fine by me. I just hoped you appreciated what a big honour that was. How much it meant to him.'

'I did,' said Luke.

'I came up here to ask you to come home,' said Lawson.

Luke wasn't game to look up at Lawson's face. Home. He had called it *home*. 'Did Annie make you come up here?'

'Nobody makes me do anything, Luke, you should know that.' Lawson looked at him. 'Annie doesn't know where you are. If she did, she'd be here herself.'

Luke kept his eyes down. He didn't want Lawson to read his face, read how desperately he wanted to come home. He had more to negotiate. 'I don't want to be a foster kid anymore. I want a job. Not just some crappy job – I could do that up here. I want to be a farrier.'

Lawson nodded. 'You got it, Luke. You'd be a bloody good farrier.'

'I would,' said Luke, nodding and frowning and not sure if he should laugh or not. He took his first swig of beer and felt it swirl around in his empty gut. He was so hungry, he skulled the whole glass.

Lawson's eyes were still on him. 'Liquid breakfast?'

Luke nodded, embarrassed. Then he burped and laughed.

26

LAWSON DROPPED LUKE at the front gates of Harry's place. 'I nearly forgot,' he said as he pulled the handbrake on. He opened the centre console and drew out a milky white stone on a string of leather. 'This yours?'

'Where'd you find that?' Luke reached out a hand and took it.

'You left it in Bob's ute.'

'When did you see *him*?'

Lawson just winked. 'I'll stop by later, okay, I'm going to go home and have a scrub.' He twisted around and looked through the rear window. 'Then you can hose out the back of my ute.'

'Yeah, sorry about that,' said Luke. 'They don't travel well.' He unclipped Fang, then moved to the other side of the ute. 'Ugh, Filth,' he muttered as he unclipped the bouncing yellow pup. 'That's *disgusting!*'

It was weird walking through the front gate. The place was empty. There were no cars in the garage and the stable doors were all open. Wind whistled over the sand in the arena. Horses grazed in the small day yards and Luke could see right down the laneway to the mares' paddock, where new foals stood sleepily beside their mothers.

A familiar whinny brought a big smile to his face. 'Legsy!'

The big black colt walked over to the fence and whinnied again.

'Hey,' said Luke. 'How are you, old friend?' With the pups at his heels, he slipped through the fencing rails and ran his hands up either side of the colt's neck, then wrapped his arms around him and breathed in his salty, horsey smell.

'You been on holidays?' asked Luke, standing back and running his eyes over Legs. He hadn't been ridden for a while, that was for sure. He was fatter and his feet were unshod and chipped around the edges.

Fang rumbled a low-pitched growl just before Luke heard the clink of the front gate. He spun around.

Grace opened the gate and led a horse through without noticing Luke.

She wasn't the first person he wanted to see. He'd been horrible to her.

He waited for her to turn around.

'Hi, Grace.'

'Luke! Where did you come from?'

'Just got here a few minutes ago.'

'Does Annie know you're here?'

'Not yet.'

Awkward silence.

'There's been people here, asking heaps of questions, looking for you. The police have been here, too. Everyone wants to know where you are.'

Luke didn't say anything. Hadn't Lawson told anyone where he was?

'We're not going to let them take you away,' said Grace, fierce determination in her voice.

'I'm not going to let them take me, either,' said Luke. 'I'm here on my own terms this time.'

'How do you mean?'

'I asked Lawson for a job. They'll probably let me stay if I can show them I've got a way to support myself.' He paused. 'I won't be just a foster kid anymore. I'll be an apprentice farrier.'

Grace looked down at her boots. 'I'm so sorry, Luke. I never should have said what I did. I feel like everything's all my fault. Everyone's been so mad at me.'

'No way, Gracie,' said Luke. 'I was such a pig. I'm really sorry.'

Grace looked up. She was crying. 'You're not mad at me?'

Luke shook his head and wondered if he should hug her or something. She was really starting to blubber.

'Umm, do you want a hug or something?'

Grace dropped the reins of the horse she was leading and hugged him hard, pinning his arms to his sides. Luke stood there. 'It's okay, Gracie. It's okay,' he said. He put his chin on the top of her head. Had she shrunk or had he grown taller?

Grace hugged him for a while until she saw Filth and Fang.

'Oh my God, look at these cute little puppies!' Grace dropped to her knees and held out her arms. They jumped all over her, waggling their scrawny bums and licking her face.

'Kworr, that one's got bad breath! What you been eating, hey, fella? What you been eating? Yes, what you been *eating*, you're so *cuuute*!'

'Fish guts,' said Luke. 'And other unmentionable things.'

'Yuck, you stinky little boy!' said Grace, roughing Filth all over, much to the pup's delight.

'Watch he doesn't pee on you.'

A car door slammed.

'Luke? Luke, is that you?' Annie got out of Lawson's

ute and hurried down the path. 'Luke! Good God, where have you been?'

He didn't even tell Annie?

Annie gave him a frail hug. She had lost so much weight. She was tiny. He hugged her back. 'Hi, Annie.'

She held his face in her hands. 'Let me look at you. Have you been looking after yourself and eating properly? You've grown another foot! You're getting so tall!'

Then she saw his arm. 'What happened to your arm?'

'Chasing brumbies,' Luke grinned.

She rolled her eyes.

Lawson appeared behind her with a stern look on his face. He was freshly shaven and had changed into a clean set of clothes. He nodded at Luke without smiling.

Luke nodded back.

'What you been up to?' said Lawson.

'Oh, hunting crocs, wrestling buffalo, that sort of thing,' shrugged Luke. 'You know how it is.'

Lawson smirked. He was having trouble keeping that straight face, Luke was sure.

'Find any brumbies?'

'Yeah, had to let them go.'

'That's a shame.'

'It was.'

'Probably some good blood running through some of them. They mix with the station horses, get the hardiness of the brumbies mixed with the good working bloodlines.'

'Yeah, well,' Luke mumbled. They had already talked about this on the way home. Lawson knew the brumbies were gone, so why was he bringing it up again?

'Go to any drafts?'

Luke nodded. 'Just a small one, rough cattle.'

Lawson's grin grew. 'Pick up your winnings?'

'No, they . . .'

He heard the hiss of brakes, and the double clutch of a truck coming down a gear as it groaned around the bend further up the road.

'Probably would have paid for some transport costs,' said Lawson. He was really struggling with that smirk. 'Course, you gotta know who to talk to about that sort of thing. They can't hand prize money over to just anyone.'

'What transport costs?'

Lawson shrugged and walked towards the front gate. A large truck wheezed as it came to a stop in front of the property. He walked stolidly out into the road, grabbed hold of the side of the truck with one hand and jumped up. He looked inside and then jumped down again to wave the truck through the gates. 'Back her up to the loading ramp, mate,' he called to the driver.

Luke's heart leapt into his throat. He pointed to the truck. 'Is that . . . ?'

Lawson raised an eyebrow and began to open the back gate of the truck.

No way . . .

Rusty came out first, slipping and sliding down the ramp, calling to the other horses behind him. The two yearlings followed and then came a tiny, bleating foal.

'Brumbies!' squealed Grace. 'Look at them!'

'Chocky!' said Luke, unable to believe his eyes as the big brown colt charged down the ramp, biting at the rumps of those in front. 'How did you get him? He was—'

Lawson slapped him on the shoulder. 'Ask Bob.'

Luke looked into the back at the truck. The driver, a rotund little man with a comb-over and tight shorts, got out and slammed the door. He walked up to Luke with an electronic gadget in his hand.

'Was there a brown mare?' Luke asked him.

'You the owner?'

Luke looked at Lawson, unsure. Lawson nodded.

'Yep,' Luke said.

'Your mate asked me to tell you the brown mare died. The foal presented breach and they had to choose between the mare and the foal. He said to say sorry, he did the best he could. I've been stopping and trying to bottle-feed her along the way, but she hasn't drunk much. Poor little thing. Didn't think she'd make it, but she's here.'

'Okay, thanks.' Luke took the gadget and scribbled

a left-handed signature on the screen with a plastic pen. 'I'll look after your baby for you, Brownie,' he said as he looked at the tiny foal. She was pathetically small, all elbows and knees, ribs poking out from under her dull coat.

'I'll help you look after her,' said Grace. 'Oh, she looks so little and hungry. Can we call her Tinkerbell?'

'*Tinkerbell*? Pfft, girls and horses,' Luke mumbled, as he looked at the wretched thing. 'You can call her anything you like if she survives.'

'I'll go and ring Dad and ask him to bring us some formula,' said Grace, jumping off the fence and running to the house.

'She's a brumby, she'll pull through,' said Lawson, hopping up on the yard rails and looking in. Rusty ran up to the other two yearlings and began bleating like a goat. He was small and skinny, and his head was too big for his body. He was not an impressive horse by any stretch of the imagination. Chocky trotted past him, big, muscular and proud. His belly tightened as he let out an impressive roar and chased up the two fillies, herding them all into a tight bunch.

Luke noticed a glow in Lawson's eyes as he watched Chocky move around the yard.

'He's got it all, that horse,' Lawson said, almost to himself.

Lawson had a thing about brumbies, Luke was beginning to realise.

Beyond the yards, Legsy roared back at the strange new colt in the yards. Then a long authoritative scream rang from the stables as Biyanga joined in.

'Lot of testosterone around here,' Luke commented.

'Yeah, I was just wondering about that,' said Lawson. 'What are you going to do with that brown colt?'

'Chocky?' Luke had no idea what he would do with any of them. He'd never expected to see the brumbies again, least of all Chocky. Bob must have known the rodeo contractors up there and got him thrown in on the deal.

'Wanna sell him?' asked Lawson.

'Maybe,' said Luke. Behind Lawson, he could see Legsy, big, black and magnificent, cantering about and shaking his long impressive mane. A crazy, far-flung idea came to his head. 'But I don't want money.'

Lawson followed Luke's eyes to Legsy and snorted. 'He's a valuable horse; reckon that'd be a fair swap?' The undertone in his voice said, *you're dreaming*.

'Yep,' said Luke. Big horse dream. Big dream horse. It was worth a shot.

Lawson glared at him.

Luke glared right back and shrugged. 'Where else are you going to get a brumby from?'

'Righto, fair swap.'

'Really?' Luke nearly fell off the fence.

'Yeah, the old man would have liked you to have him.'

'Reckon?'

'I know it. We read his will last week.'

'Legsy's mine? Harry left me Legsy?'

Lawson smiled and nodded. 'He suits you, bro.' He held out a hand to shake.

Luke took it, plaster and all, shook it hard and stared into Lawson's face. 'So is that how it's going to be?'

'What?'

'Are you my brother or not?'

'Course I am. Now piss off and get that colt worked. He hasn't been out of that paddock since the day you left.'

'But . . . the foal . . . Tinkerbell . . .'

'You've all but given her to Grace now,' Lawson chuckled. 'The foal will be fine. Go and ride your new horse.'

Luke looked at the listless foal in the yard. 'What if she doesn't drink?'

'Gracie'll take care of her.'

Luke knew he was right. Grace had raised more foals than he ever had. Tinkerbell was in good hands. He leapt off the yard rail. 'Wahoo!' he hollered, and ran to the stables. He grabbed the first bridle he could find and ran to Legsy's paddock.

'Legsy! Here, boy!'

The colt cantered up and nearly stuffed his head into the bridle by himself, opening his mouth and chomping at the bit. Luke laughed as he buckled it up, kicked off his boots, and vaulted up onto him bareback. 'Haven't you been out for a while, buddy?'

'I'm going down the river for a swim,' he yelled as he trotted Legsy down the laneway past Lawson and Annie. He couldn't wait to feel that cool water wash over him and to look up through the coachwood leaves. The colt broke into a canter and Luke grabbed hold of a piece of mane. Legsy skipped and pigrooted, squealing happily, as the pups yapped and raced behind them.

27

OUT ON THE river flats, Luke kicked Legsy into a gallop and let him stretch his legs, leaping over thick long grass in big jumps. He ducked as they cantered into the tree-lined creek, splashed through the water and trotted up the other side.

Luke let go of the reins and ripped the football jersey off his back, letting it fly up into the air behind him and disappear into the grassy flats.

When he reached the swimming hole, he dived off the colt's back and rolled around in the water, ducking under, swimming as far as he could without air and coming up again. The river was like wine.

He rolled over and floated on his back, staring up through the trees. Bands of blinding silver light streaked through the leaves, bouncing off the water that rippled over his chest. He ran his hands over his ribs.

A rumbling noise grew beyond the trees: the vibration

of horses' hooves over soft earth. The coachwood leaves jangled with the tremors.

Luke lifted his head from the water and grabbed for the colt's reins. He heard shrill cries, laughter. Filth and Fang yapped excitedly.

'*Luke!*'

'Where are you, Luke?'

'COOOO-EEE!'

Luke stood waist-deep in the water. The sound of his name wrapped in such familiar voices made him smile from ear to ear. He began wading out to the bank. 'Over here!'

A throng of horses and people galloped towards the swimming hole.

Tom was the first to burst through the trees on Nosey. The horse was gleaming with sweat and looked fit and muscular. Legsy squealed at him.

'Where've you been?' Tom demanded, slipping off and tying Nosey to a tree.

'Up in the Gulf,' grinned Luke. He couldn't wait to tell him all about it.

Shara came next on Rocko, ducking as she rode under a branch and straight into the river. 'Hi, Luke,' she said. 'About time you got back. Jess has been pining for you.'

Rosie followed shortly after on Buster. And behind her, on Buster's rump, was Jess, barefoot, wearing shorts and an old singlet, her arms around Rosie's waist, laughing.

Jess slipped off the side of the horse, dragging Rosie with her, and they both landed in a giggling heap in the sand as Buster snorted and shied sideways. 'Whoa, Buster,' said Rosie, reaching up and grabbing for the reins.

Tom ran towards Luke, dived on him, grabbed his head and tried to shove him under the water.

'I wouldn't do that if I were you . . .'

Fang immediately went on the attack, pouncing into the water and clamping his jaws around Tom's neck with ferocious high-pitched snarls.

'It's trying to kill me!' shrieked Tom, pulling at the wet, stinky black thing. 'Where'd you get the wolves from?'

Luke helped him pry the pup loose. 'You're going to have to treat me with a bit more respect now, Tom,' he joked.

'Oh, what cute puppies,' said Jess, rolling over in the sand and clapping her hands to them. 'Where did they come from? Are they yours?'

'Yep,' said Luke. 'I seem to be theirs, anyway. Meet Fang and Filth.'

Both pups promptly jumped all over her, wiggling. 'They're adorable,' said Jess.

'They need worming,' grumbled Tom, running his hand around the toothmarks on his throat.

They all swam in the river and swung off the old tyre for hours. Between swims, Shara and Jess amused themselves by burying the pups up to their necks in the coarse river sand and seeing which one could break out the fastest. Fang won every time.

Luke and Tom jumped out of tree branches and dive-bombed into the river, splashing everyone. Rosie sat up on a rock, keeping dry and painting her toenails.

Luke eventually pulled himself out of the water and plonked himself on the sand a short distance from the girls, flicking water out of his hair and catching his breath. Filth and Fang waggled their way over to him and ran their heads under his hands.

'Hey, little runt,' he said, giving Filth a cuff on the head. 'What do you think of the Coachwood River? Reckon it might be a good place to stop a while? You like all this attention, don't you.'

Jess crawled through the sand and knelt in front of Luke.

'So did the moonstone work?'

He picked the stone up from his throat and looked down at it. 'Yeah, it did. Want it back?'

She shook her head, grinning at him.

'What?'

She laughed. 'What have you been doing to yourself? You look like you've been through a cheese grater.'

'Oh, yeah that,' said Luke, looking down at his legs. 'Spinifex, it's lethal.'

'It's all over your back too. And your arms,' she noted. 'What happened?'

'I was chasing a helicopter.'

She seemed to find that hysterically funny. 'Did you catch it?'

He laughed too. Looking back, it was always going to be futile. 'No.'

'What happened to your arm?'

'Took a bit of a tumble,' he said holding the plaster up.

She twirled her finger around like a propeller. 'Chasing . . .'

He nodded. '. . . helicopters.'

'What about that?' Jess pointed to the cut on his shoulder.

Luke looked down at it. The scab was messy, but it was healing. He grinned as he thought of Tyson.

'Knife fight. Big hairy guy wanted to have a go.'

Jess looked shocked. 'Really?'

Luke shrugged, nodded and tried to look nonchalant. 'I got him first.'

'With a real knife?'

Luke nodded. 'Uh-huh.'

Jess's eyes were running all over him, but for the first

time in his life he didn't care. He looked straight back at her. She was little, with golden-brown hair and huge green eyes. Her legs were covered with sand.

'And that?' she asked, indicating the slash across the back of his hand.

'Found a brumby in a barbed wire trap. I was trying to help her.'

'*Barbed wire*? Did you get it out?'

He shook his head. 'She had a little foal too; it was sad.'

Her expression changed. 'Did it live?'

'Yeah, it did – all the other brumbies in the mob took care of him. It was amazing. I couldn't stop watching them. Still can't,' Luke smiled. 'He's in the yards at Harry's.'

Jess's face lit up. 'You brought brumbies home?'

'Yeah, you gotta come up and see them. There's an orphan foal too.'

'And you've been sitting around under trees watching them all day, huh?'

'Yeah, like some other idiot I know,' he teased. 'Least it wasn't for a whole year.'

'What about this?' she asked, taking his hand in hers and turning it over. There was a big long cut where the fishing line had sliced. She ran her finger along it and then looked at him, waiting for an answer.

Luke smiled as he thought of Toby.

'Croc got on my handline. Fought like a bastard, swishing and fighting; it wanted to death-roll me and jam me under a rock so my guts rotted.'

A suspicious look came over Jess's face. 'Right. And what about that?' She pointed to the lumps that ran down his left side.

'Wrestling water buffalo,' he said, without missing a beat. 'Got me a beauty.' He gave his ribs a pat and shook his head, whistling through his teeth, 'Geez, it hurt.'

Jess screwed up her nose and shoved Luke's shoulder so hard he reeled over backwards. 'There's no water buffalo in Queensland!'

'There is!' he insisted. 'Heaps of them, all migrating over the border from the Northern Territory! Climate change – it's really bad up there!'

'You're so full of it!' She shoved him again.

'It's true! They're like the polar bears of the Northern Territory; all their land is—' He cracked up. '—melting!'

Jess raised her eyebrows at him. 'The Northern Territory is melting.'

Luke raised his shoulders and tried to look indifferent. 'Or freezing, or something. There's some seriously pissed-off water buffalo up there, anyway.'

Jess put her hands on her hips and pulled a seriously doubtful expression.

Luke jumped up and tackled her, wrapping his arms

234

around her waist and hoisting her into the air with a roar.

She squealed noisily as he ran straight for the water and plunged in. The water crashed around and swallowed them both. He sank under the water; bubbles trickled up around his face and he could see arms and legs, flailing about. Pushing his feet off the sandy riverbed, he shot up through the surface of the water, shaking his head and laughing.

Jess bobbed up, gasping and spluttering. She pushed a wave of water right at his face with the flat of her hand.

Luke dodged and kept his eyes locked on her. 'What's your dad's name again?'

Jess looked confused. 'Craig, why?'

'Nothing.'

The sound of a small motorbike puttered beyond the trees. It grew louder as it got closer.

Elliot Duggin, the vet's youngest son, appeared on a Peewee 50 and the mood of the whole place changed instantly. Jess nearly walked on water. She paddled her arms desperately and rushed to the river's edge.

Elliot, small with geeky glasses and a shirt buttoned up to his throat, pulled off his big red helmet.

'What? What is it?' Jess demanded, grabbing for her towel.

'I've been looking everywhere for you,' said Elliot. 'Marnie's started to foal!'

Jess threw her towel on the ground. 'Oh my God, it's time! It's coming!' She began running.

'Take the colt, Jess!' Luke yelled after her.

But she kept running, straight across the river flats, barefoot with her wet hair slapping down her back.

28

WHEN LUKE REACHED the others, Marnie was lying down outside the paddock. Lawson was at her head and John Duggin was at her tail end. Jess was pacing frantically nearby while Shara tried to calm her down.

'You kids, take your horses up to the stables,' said Lawson. He pointed at Luke and waved him over.

Luke dismounted and handed his reins to Tom. He walked quietly over and crouched down near the mare. She groaned and lifted her head up off the ground, her legs going stiff and her whole body shuddering.

'How long's she been down?'

'About forty minutes,' said Lawson with a frown. 'It's backwards.'

Luke looked to the mare's back end. John was up to his elbow in horse. Sweat rolled down his face. 'I can find its tail,' he grunted. 'If I could just get both its hind legs . . .' He grimaced and pushed deeper.

Lawson pulled his keys from his pocket and tossed them to Luke. 'You know where I keep my gun,' he said in a low voice. 'Grab it and put it in the back of my ute when the girls aren't looking and drive it down here. Tell the others to stay up at the stables. The fewer people here the better.'

'What for?' asked Luke.

There was a long, high-pitched whinny from the creek and Luke whipped his head around. A flash of brilliant white appeared between the trees and then disappeared. Chelpie.

'For that thing. I've had it with her,' said Lawson. 'Now, go.'

Luke began running up the hill towards Lawson's small blue house. He could hear a horse thrashing about in the creek.

At the stables, he took Grace aside. 'Chelpie's out again,' he said. 'Lawson just asked me to get his gun. Can you go grab it from the house, put it in the ute and take it down to him. I'm going to go and see if I can catch her before he shoots her.'

Grace looked horrified.

'See if you can stall for time,' said Luke.

Grace nodded and walked smartly towards the house.

Luke grabbed a halter, locked the pups in a stable and headed for the river.

Chelpie was going nuts. She smashed between the trees, screaming and whinnying. Even from a distance, Luke could see that her ribs stuck out terribly. Her rump sagged like an old tent and her belly was huge.

He ran after her. 'Chelpie! Here, girl.'

The white mare spun and rushed at him, her teeth bared. Luke jumped behind a tree. 'Hey, what's got into you?'

Then Chelpie cantered off again and he saw. Her tail and hind legs were covered in blood.

'You've had a foal! Where is it?'

He could hear Chelpie ahead, screaming frantically, and he scrambled after her along the creek towards the Pettilows' place. After following her for several minutes, he came out onto the river flats near the Pettilow property.

Katrina came into view, walking across the flats with a halter in her hand. 'Chelpie! Come here!' She bolted for the safety of the fenceline when Chelpie galloped at her.

'She's just crazy!' Luke heard her complain angrily. 'I can't catch her!'

On the hillside, under the trees, a man worked with a shovel. 'Just get the stupid animal back in here before she causes any more trouble,' he said, without breaking from his digging . . . or *burying*? Luke spotted a gun leaning against a nearby tree.

Chelpie cantered along the fenceline, whinnying. Katrina jumped back away from her.

Luke walked calmly towards them across the field. Chelpie spotted him and trotted straight at him with her ears flat back.

Luke stood passively and let Chelpie come to him. She stopped in front of him and put her nose in his lap. 'Chelpie,' he said gently. 'What happened?'

The little mare nickered softly, then gave a long, sad whinny. He put the rope around her neck and then slid the halter over her ears. 'Easy, girl.'

Katrina marched over to him. 'I'll take her,' she said, holding her hand out for the rope.

'What happened?' asked Luke.

'Nothing. It's none of your business.' Katrina yanked at Chelpie's rope.

Luke kept hold of it. 'Did she lose a foal or something?'

'No.' Katrina pulled harder.

Luke refused to let go. 'Come on, Katrina, she's got blood all over her. What's your dad burying over there?'

'This horse has exceptional breeding and has had a very successful show career. We hand-raised her since she was a two-day-old foal. You don't think I'm going to just let her have a foal to some mongrel-bred stockhorse, do you?'

'What mongrel-bred stockhorse?'

Katrina scoffed and pulled at the rope. 'You work it out.'

Luke let the rope go and Katrina led Chelpie back to the paddock. The mare pulled at the halter but Katrina held her firmly. He thought of Marnie on the other side of the creek, foaling, on the same day.

Muscles got Chelpie too. That night, in Longwood!

Then he thought of the brumbies, circling the dead red mare.

'Poor Chelpie,' he said quietly. 'They didn't even let you say goodbye.' Then Katrina's words rung in his ears. *We hand-raised her since she was a two-day-old foal.* So Chelpie had been a potty foal. 'They didn't even let you know your own mother?'

When Luke got back to the river flats, Marnie was standing with her hind legs stretched awkwardly behind her. John was still at her back end.

Jess was watching, two hands over her mouth.

'John thinks he's got its hind feet,' Shara told Luke. 'When the mare stood up, it slipped back in a bit and made it easier to turn.'

'I got them!' said John, his arm still inside the mare. 'I got them.' He drew out two tiny hooves, twisted together, then grabbed one in each hand, bent his knees and pulled them down towards the mare's hocks. Two legs began to slide out.

'Oh my God . . .' Jess gasped.

'He's got it now.' Shara smiled. 'It's coming, Jessy!'

Jess squeaked something unintelligible and began to hop up and down.

The mare dropped to the ground and began pushing again.

'We gotta get it out quick, Lawson,' said John. 'I need a hand.'

Lawson looked at Jess. 'Stop blubbering and go give him a hand.'

Jess hurriedly smeared the tears away. She crept to the back of the mare, sniffing and swallowing, and took a leg. The hocks came out first, emerging downwards with the mare's contractions until the foal's hindquarters appeared.

The mare stopped and rested, puffing, her eyes only half-open. Sweat soaked her flanks and her neck.

'Come on, sweet thing,' said Lawson, rubbing the mare's forehead. 'You can do this.'

'It's a chestnut. It's a filly,' Jess blubbered. 'Sharsy, it's a girl. I can see its little thingy!'

'It's not out yet, Jess,' said John. 'Half a horse is not

much good to you. Right, now we pull straight out in line with the mare's spine, okay?'

Jess nodded. It took a few more contractions before the shoulders were out and then the neck and head slipped out into a pool of water and mucus. The foal lay half-covered in a white, plasticky film, one foot still inside the mare.

'Come away now,' said John, taking Jess's arm and drawing her away.

The mare and the foal both lay there, breathing and resting.

Jess grabbed Luke's arm and squeezed it. 'I can't believe she's finally here! It's been forever!' Then she looked at his arm and saw the blood and goop she'd just smeared all over it. 'Oh, sorry.'

'No biggy. I've had worse.' He grabbed her shirt and wiped his arm on it.

'Oi!'

After a few more minutes, Marnie turned and gently sniffed her baby. The foal blinked and sniffed her back, their noses touching for a second. The mare began licking her foal, cleaning away the mucus that covered her.

'Isn't she beautiful?' said Jess. 'Her name's Opal. I named her months ago.'

But Luke didn't hear her. He was staring in disbelief at the three silver marks, perfect diamonds, that cascaded down the foal's shoulder like falling stars. 'Jess, didn't your horse Diamond have marks like that on her hindquarters?'

He turned to Jess, whose mouth had dropped open. She was staring disbelievingly at the glistening wet foal. 'What?' she asked in a distracted voice.

'I said, didn't Diamond have marks like that?'

'Yes,' whispered Jess, without taking her eyes off the foal. It put one long shaky leg out in front of it, revealing more of its shoulder.

'It was the *lights*,' she whispered in awe. 'The min min lights, the ghosts, in Marnie's belly, three lights, three white stars . . .'

'Whoa, that's freaky.'

Jess grabbed Luke's hand and squeezed it. 'It's Diamond's spirit! The min min lights, remember?'

You've got dream there, you and this Jess girl.

Luke couldn't get Tyson's voice out of his head. He wouldn't have believed it if he hadn't seen it with his own eyes.

There was a shrill whinny from the river and everyone turned. A flash of white darted through the trees. Chelpie came cantering up over the river flats with a rope dangling between her front legs.

Jess groaned. 'Not *her* again.'

Marnie jumped to her feet and Lawson had just enough time to grab her halter before she charged at Chelpie. Opal lay on the ground and called a tiny whinny to her mother.

'Did you get that gun, Luke? asked Lawson.

'Get out of here, you evil thing,' screamed Jess. 'You've already killed one of my horses. You're not getting this one!'

'She's not evil,' said Luke, running out towards the mare. 'She's just lost a foal.' He took Chelpie's halter and tried to calm her by running his hand up and down her neck. She nickered anxiously. 'She thinks Opal's her foal.'

'Get her out of here, she's upsetting the mare,' Lawson snapped.

Luke turned Chelpie and tried to lead her away. She reared up and struck at him, and as she did, Luke saw milk running down either side of her hind legs. 'You poor thing,' he said, holding her firmly.

Then an idea came to him. 'Come on, Chelpie,' he said, turning her about. 'There's someone back at Harry's place you might like to meet.'

That night, Luke slid through his bedroom window and slipped across the courtyard. Filth whimpered. Fang yapped and growled. He unclipped them from their night chains and then snuck in through the back door to the stables with them padding softly behind him. He heard

Legsy snoring. Biyanga shook his head over the half door, ruffling his mane.

Outside, the brumbies nickered softly to each other. Luke walked out into the night and leaned on the rails of the yard to check on them.

A small, smiling moon cast dappled light through the old coachwood tree. He could see Rusty standing next to Chocky with a low head and a resting leg, looking sleepy. The fillies raised their heads and pricked their ears.

Luke walked to the next yard and poked his head over. A rush of white, gleaming in the moonlight, charged at him with a full set of teeth. Chelpie swung around and double-barrelled the fence, connecting with a bang so hard it almost rattled the pins from the rails. She trotted back to Tinkerbell, nuzzling and nickering protectively. Then she stood between Luke and the filly with a leg raised in warning, ears flat back.

Luke smiled. 'Don't worry, girl, I won't let them take this one away from you. Not for a while, anyway.'

Luke had talked the Pettilows into leaving Chelpie in his care until she calmed down a bit. All it had taken to convince them was six months of free feed and agistment, and an agreement not to ride her. Unbeknown to the Pettilows, and with only a small dose of sedative, Luke had managed to settle Chelpie enough to introduce her to her new baby.

Tinkerbell nickered and Chelpie nuzzled the filly to her belly, offering her milk. The little foal tottered around and butted at her udder.

'Bunch of little foster kids,' said Luke quietly as he looked at all the horses in the yards. 'You've come to the right place.'

He walked to the feedroom, gathered up the horse rugs and took them out to the stable aisle. There he made a cosy nest, flinging straps and buckles out of the way, and flopped himself down in the middle, jockeying for position with Filth and Fang.

He lay back and thought of Marnie's little red filly with the three diamonds cascading down its shoulder like falling stars. Then of Tinkerbell the orphaned brumby foal, nuzzled up with Chelpie, the show pony with impeccable breeding and faultless conformation.

And as he lay there thinking, listening to the familiar, soothing sounds of home, there was a soft, flapping noise above him and a dark shape glided across the top of the building to land on a crossbeam. A big owl looked around the building. Luke smiled up at its tawny-brown dinnerplate face.

'We're all just the same, aren't we?' he said to the bird. 'Same way my mob. Same way your mob.' He shrugged. 'Same way that horse mob.'

The owl sat silently with a shrewd look on its face

for a while longer. Then it shook its feathers, lifted its wings and glided off through the western window into the darkness.

Acknowledgements

To Tyson Kaawoppa Yunkaporta, for your advice,
encouragement and wonderful ideas, thank you from
the bottom of my heart.

Thanks also to my wonderful and adventurous
friend Suzanne Sandral, for showing me the Gulf.

And to my perfect husband, Anthony, thanks for
your never-ending love and support.

About the Author

KAREN WOOD has been involved with horses for more than twenty years. After owning many horses, she has finally found her once-in-a-lifetime-horse in a little chestnut stockhorse called Reo. Karen has an Arts degree majoring in communications and a diploma in horticulture. She has syndicated a gardening column in several newspapers throughout Australia, has published feature articles in various magazines and has published photographs in bushwalking guides. She is married with two children and lives on the Central Coast, New South Wales.

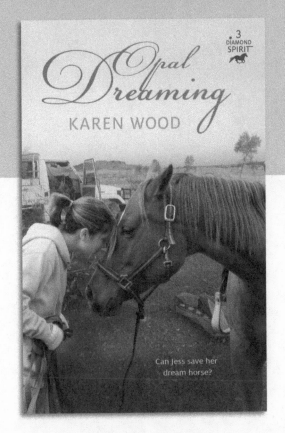

3

DIAMOND
SPIRIT

Opal Dreaming

KAREN WOOD

Can Jess save her
dream horse?

A SNEAK PREVIEW

OF THE THIRD BOOK IN THE DIAMOND SPIRIT SERIES

'*WOOHOO!*' JESS SLID DOWN the front stair rail, her arms out wide, and landed expertly on the driveway. 'Today's the day!'

For the first time in weeks, the sky was a clear blue, and the air was still, not a breath of wind. The sun was warm on Jess's face and everything about the day seemed perfect. She skipped to the feed shed, hauled out some hay and threw it over the fence. 'Come on, Dodger, it's time to go and get Opal!'

Dodger nickered to her and began snuffling at the hay. Jess stepped through the fence and gave the old stock-horse a big hug. 'Eighteen months we've been waiting,' she said, running her hands through his shaggy brown coat. 'I can't *believe* I can finally bring her home!'

She took a brush to him, rubbing in hard circular motions as she talked. 'Opal's a very special filly. She's connected to Diamond. You remember Diamond, don't you?'

As Jess rubbed Dodger's back, the old horse curled his lip with pleasure. She combed out his tail, painted his hooves with grease, and pulled her phone from her pocket to thumb a message.

U guys saddled yet?

Before she could send it, Jess heard a shrill '*Coo-ee!*' A clatter of hooves sounded along the road, gradually getting louder. From behind the hedge, she could hear her friends, chatting and laughing.

'I thought you'd have that old stockhorse saddled up by now,' Shara called as she rode through the gate on Rocko.

'Sharsy!' Jess squealed. 'You're home!' The day was becoming more perfect by the minute.

'Dad brought me home for the weekend,' her best friend grinned.

'How's vet school?'

'I'm their star student!'

Rosie followed on her quarter horse. 'You're back on the legend, Jessy!' she said, as she pulled Buster to a halt and jumped off.

Jess gave Dodger a pat on the neck. 'I will be in a minute.' She picked up her new stock saddle and slung it over his back, pulled the girth through the rig and slapped the fenders down into place.

'Are you excited?' asked Grace, appearing on a leggy chestnut.

'I couldn't sleep last night,' answered Jess, as she reached for her bridle.

'Have you got a little halter for her?' asked Shara.

'We don't need one. We're just going to lead the mare and let Opal follow.'

'What? All the way back to here without a halter?' Shara sounded mildly alarmed.

'Probably the best way. She's never been touched by a human, let alone had a rope on her,' said Jess. She pulled a face. '*Lawson's rules.*'

As part of the purchase agreement with Lawson, Jess had agreed not to handle Opal during her first six months. Lawson didn't like foals being mollycoddled by girls. He said it made them 'rude and disrespectful'.

Shara snorted. 'He's such a killjoy.'

'Not for much longer,' said Jess. 'As soon as she's weaned, she'll be *mine*! I'll have three whole weeks to handle her before she goes out west to Longwood.'

'Wish *we* could go on that trip,' said Grace.

Lawson had inherited a share in his father's grazing property, Blakely Downs, and was taking several horses, including a mob of brumbies, out there for a droving trip. Opal, together with the other young horses, would be turned out onto the station to fatten up on the Mitchell grass. The older horses would be put to work on the stock route, droving fifteen hundred cattle to the saleyards.

'Me too,' Jess sighed. 'Droving would be so much fun.' She rammed a foot into a stirrup and sprang into the saddle.

'Are you leaving Opal's mum with her for a couple of days?' asked Shara.

'Yeah, just overnight to get her settled, then Lawson wants to get Marnie back into work for the droving trip.'

'You'd better look after her,' said Rosie. 'Do you have any idea how much he paid for that mare?'

'Mum reckons it was enough to buy a brand-new car,' said Grace.

'She'll be all right,' said Jess. 'Lawson's been over and checked the fences to make sure she can't hurt herself.'

At that moment a low rumbling noise rolled through the valley, making the ground tremble.

'What was that?' asked Jess, looking up at the cloudless blue sky.

'Storm,' said Grace. 'It's supposed to come through later this afternoon.'

'Look, the sky's turning green over there,' said Shara, pointing beyond the mountains to the south. 'It's gonna be a doozy!'

Jess gathered her reins and kicked Dodger on. 'Let's get going. We don't want to get stuck in it.'

The girls headed towards the river flats. As they followed a well-worn track to the crossing, they could hear thunder rumbling through the valley again.

'That sky's getting darker,' warned Rosie.

'It's coming up over the hills,' said Shara. 'Look!' Behind Mossy Mountain, the sky was turning an eerie mix of green and purple. It suddenly flashed white with the afterglow of distant lightening. 'We're going to get drenched.'

'I don't care – I love riding in the rain,' said Grace.

'So do I, but I hope it doesn't unsettle Opal while we're trying to move her,' said Jess.

Grace scoffed. 'Horses aren't scared of rain.'

'But what if the river rises?' Jess squeezed Dodger into a trot. 'We might not be able to get her through. I couldn't handle having to wait until next weekend to bring her home.'

Dodger swished his tail and gave a skip with a hind leg. He broke into a canter. Jess led the girls down the river-bank and they splashed through the knee-deep water.

Shara cantered up on her shoulder. 'Can't that old gerry go any faster?' she yelled, as she thundered past.

Dodger seized the bit and took off after Rocko, with Buster and Milly following closely behind. Jess gave him the reins and let him stretch his legs. It felt fantastic to be flying along on him again, his hooves making a loud melodic rumble over the grassy flats. She laughed into the wind and kicked him on.

Beyond the grassy flats at the Slaughtering Creek junction, the group reached Katrina Pettilow's place. Her horse Chelpie stood listlessly on a timbered hillside. When the little white mare saw the girls, she pulled a horrible face and charged at the fence.

'Have they weaned Tinkerbell already?' asked Shara, pulling Rocko back to a walk.

'About a month ago,' said Jess. 'Katrina wanted Chelpie back.'

'Did she ever find out about Tinks?'

'Nope. She didn't visit Chelpie once in six months.' Jess shook her head. Her friend Luke had used Chelpie to foster his orphan brumby filly when Chelpie had lost her own foal. The little mare had been a good mother, ferociously protective. 'She's done nothing but pace up and down that fence since Tinks was taken away from her. She looks terrible.'

'Look how skinny she is,' Shara said in disgust.

'Katrina should sell her if she's not interested in her anymore,' said Rosie. 'Poor horse.'

'Chelpie's so sour. Who'd buy her?' said Jess. 'I just wish Katrina would feed her a bit more.'

She looked up at the bank of thick cloud that was swelling behind the mountains – it was moving unbelievably fast – and pushed Dodger into a trot. Chelpie called a screeching whinny as they departed.

The weather caught up with them just as they rode around the bend alongside the old sawmill. Heavy drops speared into their oilskin jackets and rolled down their helmets. Up ahead, Lawson's blue timber house stood as neat as a pin. Perfectly straight fences radiated from brick stables and, in the paddocks, the mango trees were heavy with ripening fruit.

The girls walked the horses through Lawson's fat red cattle dotted about the flats, then rode up the laneway and into the stable block. The rain was deafening on the tin roof, but it was warm and dry inside.

Lawson pulled himself from beneath the horse he was shoeing and stretched. 'I've got another couple of horses to trim before we can move that filly,' he shouted over the din. 'And I've gotta get the cattle in. That river's gonna rise this afternoon.'

Jess's heart sank. Opal was too little to be swimming across rivers, especially fast-flowing ones. 'Do you want *us* to bring them in?' she yelled. 'We can do it while you finish shoeing those horses.'

'Yeah, righto, just don't stir 'em up.'

Shara grinned cheekily. 'Would we do such a thing?'

Lawson frowned. 'You can go down on foot, Shara. Take a bucket of molasses and call them up. Jess, you get behind them on that old stockhorse and do a head count of forty-three.' He raised his voice in the direction of Grace, who was at the other end of the stable block, tethering her horse. 'Gracie, can you slip a halter on that grey out in the yards and bring her in? Leave the big gate open for the cattle to come through.'

Jess rode back out of the building and quickly cast her eyes around the house yard for Luke. She barely saw him now that he was working for Lawson. He was usually out in the work ute, doing the trimming jobs. When he'd worked at Harry's place, she'd always known where to find him, but these days their paths rarely crossed. Jess couldn't see the ute. He must be out again.

She rode down the laneway, Shara clomping behind her. Then, while Shara stood calling out and banging on the bucket, Jess made a wide circle around the cattle. Red and white baldy faces popped out from behind trees, and bellows came from around the bend, as the herd began to wander through the rain towards the molasses. Jess didn't need to do much but sit there and count them as they plodded by. On the other side of the river she thought she could hear Chelpie's distressed whinnying above the sound of the rain.

Jess counted thirty-nine head of cattle, with four more emerging from the bushes below, and pulled her phone from her pocket to text Shara, who she could see pouring the molasses into the yard trough.

going to check Chelpie, somethgs wrong

She watched Shara pull her phone out, thumb a message and wave to her, as she opened the gate for the cattle.

Buzz, rumble.

Shara: will get Rocko + follow u down.

Jess trotted back across the flats towards the river. The rain pelted at her and she had to keep her chin down to shield her face. As she ducked under tree branches, she could see the white pony in the distance, her hind legs pulling at the fence wire.

Typical. Wish the Pettilows would fix their fences.

As Jess approached, she saw that Chelpie's legs were caught. Jumping down from Dodger, she checked for injuries and found none, so she carefully untwisted the wire and lifted Chelpie's back feet out of the tangled mess. As she slipped off the last of the wire, the mare squealed and lashed out with both hind feet. Jess only just managed to duck, and Chelpie's hooves connected instead with Dodger's flank. Dodger jumped sideways and, finding himself loose, trotted off across the flats with his reins dangling. Chelpie cantered after him.

'Oh, don't run away,' moaned Jess. '*Dod*ger!' She pulled her phone from her pocket and messaged Shara.

can u grab D?

She tucked her phone away and stood waiting, hands on hips. Moments later, Shara emerged from the river on Rocko, leading Dodger behind her. 'What happened?' she asked. 'You okay?'

'It's the last time I help that stupid horse,' said Jess. 'Now we'll have to stuff around for hours trying to catch her.' Her boot squelched with water as she stepped into the stirrup, and a trickle of water crept under her collar and ran down her spine. Her saddle was like a wet sponge.

'She's headed towards Lawson's place,' said Shara, turning Rocko. 'Hope she doesn't make trouble.'

'Great,' mumbled Jess, as she watched Chelpie prancing about in the pouring rain with her tail in the air. 'That's all we need.'